"Stop it, Becky! You're getting hysterical!"

"Hysterical? How convenient that men always use that word when a woman is telling them things they don't want to hear."

With a jerk, Matt imprisoned her in his arms, dropping his head determinedly. He kissed her hard.

"Matt, this won't solve anything," she gasped.

"Maybe not," he agreed raspingly, "but it beats the hell out of arguing!"

ROSALIE ASH spent several years as a bilingual personal assistant before her lifelong enjoyment of writing led to her career as a novelist. Her interests include languages, travel and research for her books, reading, and visits to the Royal Shakespeare Theatre in nearby Stratford-upon-Avon, England. Other pleasures include swimming, yoga and country walks.

Marriage Vows

ROSALIE ASH

THE MARRIAGE CONTRACT

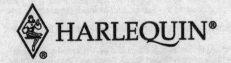

TORONTO • NEW YORK • LONDON
AMSTERDAM • PARIS • SYDNEY • HAMBURG
STOCKHOLM • ATHENS • TOKYO • MILAN • MADRID
PRAGUE • WARSAW • BUDAPEST • AUCKLAND

ISBN 0-373-80538-1

MARRIAGE VOWS

First North American Publication 2003.

CHAPTER ONE

REBECCA looked down from the terrace, and shivered.

It was him. Matt Hawke wasn't the kind of man you mistook for anyone else. Even from here, with the evening sun in her eyes, and dusk throwing violet shadows over the white walls, she knew it was him. What was more, he was heading up here, taking the steep stone steps two at a time with that familiar lazy grace—tall, powerful, lean and suntanned in a loose white T-shirt and ragged cut-off denims.

Her knuckles tightened round the edges of the tray she was carrying, and with a sudden lurch of panic she thought she was going to drop it, sending six dirty dinner-plates and assorted left-overs crashing to the floor of the crowded restaurant terrace. Forcing herself to hang grimly on to it, she retreated unsteadily into the small, circular kitchen and deposited it on one of the worktops.

'You look as if you're in shock.' Sofie glanced at her in surprise, deftly adding small sprigs of fresh tarragon to four plates of chicken in white wine sauce. 'I said you shouldn't help out, Becky! You're supposed to be *recovering*, not charging up and down the Old Mill terraces with trays!'

'*He's* here,' she whispered. Her voice sounded taut with melodrama, and she winced at her own nervous tension.

'*He*?' Her sister teased curiously, 'Who is "*he*"? King Constantine himself? The Aga Khan?'

'Matt.'

'Oh.' The response was a soundless shape of Sofie's lips. Raising her eyes heavenwards, she lifted the tray of chicken and elbowed past to deliver it to the waiting customers. 'Then, if it's anything like the old days, goodbye peace and tranquillity,' she added wryly.

Left seething in the kitchen, Becky clenched her hands into fists of frustration. She loved her sister dearly but at times she could throttle her. Now was definitely one of those times. Didn't Sofie have any idea how she felt, faced with the reappearance of Matt after two years?

One of the waiters pushed past her, and she tentatively stepped back on to the terrace. How could feeling apprehensive bring on such a feeling of physical sickness?

Like a fawn at bay, she glanced anxiously round the tables. The terraces were almost full now. It was nine-thirty, and the evening sky had abruptly changed to the velvety mauve unique to these Greek islands. In a quarter of an hour it would be pitch-dark, with the lights of Skopelos harbour—the cafés and bars, the yachts moored on the quay—dotted below them like glow-worms.

Had he come up here? Had it been him, after all? Had she hallucinated, maybe? In all honesty, she'd dreamed about him often enough these last months—bitter-sweet dreams, jumbled and confused, the wanting and the hating all churned up together into nightmares. Her heavy swath of honey-brown hair fell over one eye, and she shakily lifted her hand to push it back behind her ear.

The touch on her arm made her jump so violently that she nearly fell over.

'Hello, Becky,' said a husky, taunting voice, 'Highly-strung as ever, I see.'

She caught her breath sharply.

'Matt. What—what on earth are you *doing* here?'

'Hoping to get a meal. What else? This *is* the famous Old Mill Restaurant isn't it? Best Anglo-French cuisine in the Northern Sporades?'

'We're fully booked,' she said hoarsely.

'Then I'll just have an ouzo and wait,' he returned smoothly.

Speechless, she stared at him, and felt his dark blue eyes move speculatively over her. All around diners laughed and talked, glasses chinked, cutlery clinked. A party of Germans were laughing, and taking flash-photos of the view and of each other. An English family were bewailing the last night of their holiday, joking about missing the plane and staying on...

The relaxed atmosphere could have been in another dimension. The air between herself and Matt was so thick with tension that she could feel it enveloping her like a suffocating blanket.

In black cotton walking-shorts and V-necked black T-shirt, her hair recently washed and falling in a smooth bell past her shoulders, she knew she looked reasonably smart. But she felt awkward—too pale, too thin. She knew that he was assessing the changes in her, and sensed the amused disapproval.

'Is this the latest look in the modelling world—starving waif?' he murmured. The slow grin sent her heart-rate into overdrive. But behind the amusement lurked a smoky, repressed anger which made her shiver where she stood. He was angry with her? Why? What gave him the right to feel angry with her? She'd done him a favour, hadn't she? Quit their doomed relationship before he'd had the embarrassment and inconvenience of ending it himself?

A mixture of defiance, pride and confusion brought a flush of heat to her face. Steeling herself, she dug her hands into her pockets. 'I'm not modelling any longer.'

'No? You can't be over the hill at twenty-two?'

'You know damn well why I stopped modelling.'

'True. I assumed you'd go back to it.'

'Well, I didn't.' She gazed at his disreputable appearance, taking in the stubble-blackened chin, the tousled black hair growing in long unruly waves almost to the base of his neck. He looked like one of the sun-scorched characters off the sponge-diving boats from Lemnos. Like a pirate, fresh off his invading galleon... A stir of response made her stomach contract. Just over six feet tall, with that mesmerising petrol-blue gaze narrowed intently on her, Matt Hawke possessed an unnerving charisma which had nothing to do with his strong, hard features, or the muscular strength of his body.

'Is this the latest look for this year's ruthless company trouble-shooter?' she returned, with a touch of asperity, 'T- shirt, denims and two days' stubble?'

'I'm on holiday,' he supplied casually, grinning at the sharpness of her words. 'Don't you like the rough look, Becky?'

Where you're concerned I don't like any look, she wanted to say. Instead, she compressed her lips and turned to Vangelis, one of the young Greek waiters. 'Could you bring this *gentleman* an ouzo, please?'

The cool put-down in her words was undermined by Sofie, hurrying towards them with her empty tray.

'Matt, how lovely to see you again!' To Becky's fury, her sister went on tiptoe to kiss Matt's dark cheek, her bubbly warmth full of welcome and her short ash-blonde curls bobbing as she laughed,

'Where've you been hiding this last couple of years? Richard and I have missed you!'

'Nice to know someone has.' His smile was smoothly unreadable. 'Most of the time I've been in Hong Kong.'

'Rescuing some debt-laden business from extinction?'

'Something like that.'

'More likely sending some debt-laden business to its grave and keeping the pickings for himself,' Becky amended sweetly.

'Maybe that's a more accurate picture,' Matt agreed, without a flicker.

'Look, if you two have lots of arguing to catch up on, do me a favour and don't do it here,' Sofie pleaded, preparing to dash off to the kitchen. 'The last thing I need is a running battle between the tables!'

'*Sofie*!' Becky suppressed the urge to scream.

'She's right.' Matt nodded curtly. Suddenly the humour had gone. 'We have a lot to catch up on, Becky. Come down to the quayside and have a drink with me?'

'I'd rather die of thirst.'

'Don't be childish.'

'I'm working here tonight,' she added huskily, blushing faintly under her sister's sharp scrutiny. 'So I haven't time...'

'Take the night off,' Sofie advised quietly. Her

bright, breezy manner had faded too. The atmosphere was thick with tension, and even Sofie could sense it. 'Go and talk to Matt, Becky. Until one of you decides to do something about it, he *is* still your husband!'

The brief pause hung bleakly between them.

'So I am.' Matt's drawl was softly provocative.

Becky felt her throat dry and her palms grow damp. Panic, she recognised dimly; it did the strangest things to her. The sensation of the simultaneous physical drying and dampening briefly distracted her from the frightening prospect yawning ahead.

Matt, eerily picking up the panic signals in her silence as if the intervening months had shrunk to nothing, reached out his hand to touch her cheek, his gaze a fraction softer.

'Come on, Becky.'

His words jolted her from the paralysis of her fear.

'Don't touch me,' she snapped. 'And don't patronise me. I've done lots of growing up since we— we parted.'

'Maybe you have,' he mused, eyeing her thoughtfully, 'and maybe not.' The expression in his eyes was enigmatic, but somewhere in the shadowy blue depths lurked just a glimmer of emotion which made her pulses jolt and begin to race. This was what she'd been dreading, coward that she was. This was why she'd put off writing the letter, postponed the decision—this agonising knowledge that he affected her this way.

In apprehensive silence, she found herself following him slowly down the long, twisting flight of white-painted stone steps. The dusk was deepening. The violet air was thickening to purple all round her, and when they hit street-level she had to catch hold of the stone wall at the base of the steps as a wave of rolling, undulating dizziness briefly washed over her.

'Are you all right?' Matt's cool, deep voice held a hint of concern. She set her teeth and nodded calmly.

'Perfectly all right, thanks. I've had a virus, that's all...'

That was the only reason she was here, she wanted to add. Otherwise, she'd still be on the other side of the world, in a place where not even the all-powerful Matt Hawke could track her down...

'A virus! How long ago?'

They'd reached the start of the open-air cafés, arrayed along the broad pavement of the quayside in such close proximity that it was hard to see where one ended and another began.

'As if you cared!' Her retort was calmly challenging. They stopped at a café with low glass tables, padded wicker chairs and a glowing golden canvas awning.

'Becky—' his voice was ominously reasonable as

they chose a table nearest the water and sat down opposite each other, '—I'm beginning to feel confused. You walked out on me two years ago. Since then you've managed to sink into obscurity and avoid any contact. How, in the name of sweet hell, would you know whether I cared or not?'

She met his narrowed blue gaze for a long, shaky moment before dropping her eyes. The glitter in his held a dangerous edge.

'I don't want to talk about this,' she said tightly. 'God, I knew what it would be like. The way you—you fence everything. The way you *negotiate* everything, like one of your—your bloody business deals...'

'Becky—'

'No, that's not true,' she amended, unable to help the deepening bitterness. 'Your business deals have always been far more important than *any* personal relationship you've ever stumbled into, haven't they Matt?'

A youthful waiter had appeared, hovering politely, his dark eyes flicking appreciatively over Becky's slender, tanned thighs.

'Water for me, please.'

Matt twitched a mocking eyebrow.

'Bring us a bottle of mineral water, and two ouzos, please,' he told the waiter.

'Arrogant as ever?' she said bleakly, when the young Greek had gone.

'Naturally.' Matt's wide mobile mouth was grim. The vertical lines from his large, strong nose to the corners of his mouth had deepened slightly since she'd last seen him. They accentuated his air of world-weary cynicism. Without warning, she had a rush of memory—the devouring, uninhibited passion of that mouth on hers, the dark force of his sexual charisma sweeping away her defences, swamping her senses...

With a shiver, she hugged her arms round herself, regardless of the warm night.

'You accuse me of sinking into obscurity,' she persisted, dimly conscious of feeling goaded into unnecessary self-defence, 'but don't pretend you couldn't have found me if you'd wanted to. Don't pretend you gave a damn where I was!'

'Would you have wanted me to find you?' His cool response was somehow an unwelcome shock.

'No,' she managed, as evenly as she could. 'No. There was no point, was there?'

Matt was silent. Unwillingly she stared at him. The waiter brought their drinks, unloading the tray as the silence lengthened. She couldn't tear her eyes away from Matt.

The white T-shirt moulded the lean, smoothly muscled contours of his shoulders and chest; it clung to the ridged flatness of his stomach, and then disappeared into the waistband of his jeans. The faded denim, in turn, outlined explicitly the fullness of the male bulge of his crotch before hugging the hard shape of his lazily spread thighs. His long legs below the cut-off bermudas were strongly muscled, tanned to a dark mahogany and covered in coarse black hair. Black canvas deck-shoes completed the outfit. There was a nasty-looking cut on his shin, just healing up...

'Here.' There was a cool gleam of challenge in his eyes as he leaned forward to pour some of the mineral water into the ouzo. 'When you've finished itemising my fashion sense, have a drink. Loosen up.'

She glared at him. Short of attracting the waiter's attention to bring another glass, she was stuck with the cloudy aniseed drink, which packed a punch worthy of a heavy-weight boxer. She reached for it with a hand which shook with anger, and took a gulp.

'I warn you, if I "loosen up" I might end up saying something I'll regret.'

'Sounds interesting. In my favour, naturally?'

She decided that this didn't even merit a reply. Settling back in the wicker chair, she crossed her long legs and regarded him uncertainly over the rim of her glass.

'What happened to your leg?' She hadn't meant to ask. Matt's eyes were blank for a moment, then he glanced down as if remembering.

'I slipped on deck in a storm, about three weeks

ago. The *meltemi* wind blew up a month early. Took
me by surprise—'

'You've been sailing around the islands for three
weeks?' she cut in, frowning in bewilderment.

'A little longer,' Matt hedged smoothly. He
leaned back in his chair, flexing his powerful shoulders. The wry twist of his mouth told her that he'd
noticed her confusion.

'But I thought—' She stopped abruptly. What *had*
she thought? That he'd arrived here in person because of the letter? She'd assumed that that was why
he was here, even though the letter had been simple,
straightforward and to the point—definitely not re-
quiring a personal visit...

But if he'd been sailing for so long, there was no
guarantee that he'd received it, was there?

'Yes?' he probed softly, 'What did you think?'

'I—I thought you never took time off!' she
fenced, unconvincingly.

Matt's gaze narrowed, but he appeared to take the
remark at face value.

'I was taking time off three years ago when I met
you,' he reminded her calmly. 'Or have you forgotten already?'

'It's not a memory I cling to particularly,' she
lied, forcing her voice to stay cool.

'No? I can imagine.' There was just a trace of
bitterness in his voice. Or was she mistaken?

Despairingly, she took another large mouthful of

ouzo, and closed her eyes. The glow of the alcohol seemed to warm her all the way down inside her chest.

'Why are you here, Matt?' she managed finally. 'Why have you come to see me?'

There was a short silence.

'I didn't,' he said flatly. 'I had some business in Athens. While I was here in the Sporades I thought I'd call in and see Sofie and Richard, and who should I see scurrying around on the terrace playing at being a waitress but my devoted little runaway wife.'

'Don't patronise me, Matt!'

His grin was a slash of white against the dark of his face. But it lacked humour.

'OK. I won't patronise you. Where have you been hiding these last two years, Becky?'

'I haven't been hiding,' she told him, stiffly. 'I— I've been working abroad.'

'But not modelling?'

She shook her head. She could see him thinking, wondering what else she could possibly have managed to do. He'd always seen her as a brainless bimbo; she knew he had. He'd always treated her with the whimsical indulgence of an intelligent adult for an amusing child.

'You haven't been here—I've checked with Sofie from time to time.'

'Why?' The bitter question brought a furrow of annoyance between his eyes.

'Why?' he echoed abruptly. 'Because you're my *wife*, Becky!'

'And you like to know the whereabouts of your possessions?'

His wide mouth thinned, his face darkening a fraction.

'Precisely,' he agreed expressionlessly.

'Tell me something,' she said shakily. 'Have you been sailing round the islands alone?'

'Not all the time.'

'And have your companions been male or female?'

'Both. Which doesn't mean I've suddenly turned bisexual,' he teased mockingly. Heat crept into her cheeks, despite her efforts to stay cool and poised, and the look in his eyes was turning her heart over, making her stomach feel hollow with remembered longing.

'I can't imagine you spending a whole month at sea without some besotted female sharing your bunk,' she countered acidly.

'If you didn't want me to seek solace with some other female, Becky, why did you desert my bed?'

'You *know* why I left!' Abruptly she was seething with fury. How dared he turn up like this, and taunt her and question her about her past actions?

'I know we had a ridiculous transatlantic telephone conversation. I know you hurled a couple of dozen accusations at me based solely on the deranged scribblings of some fruit-cake of a woman I'd scarcely even spoken to…'

Becky was shaking her head angrily, her eyes closed.

'Stop it—stop it! Stop raking it all up again as if…as if it can be rationalised and dismissed, just because two years have gone by! You know you were partying and—and flirting in Hong Kong…you know you were! You and Su-Lin were meant to marry before I appeared on the scene. I was just an unfortunate…deviation!'

Matt stared at her for a long moment, his dark face unreadable. Finally he shook his head slowly.

'In the face of such jealous certainty, what can a man say?'

She glared at him, suddenly trembling with fury.

'Listen, Matt, I don't know what you want. I don't understand why you're here—'

'And I've never known what you want,' he cut in coolly. 'I've never understood what goes on in that insecure little head of yours, Rebecca.'

She found herself nervously fiddling with a strand of her honey-brown hair, twisting it into a corkscrew ringlet around her forefinger.

'Nothing, of course,' she reminded him, with wide-eyed innocence. 'Don't you remember? You married an empty-headed bimbo for the sole reason that she was stupid enough to get herself pregnant just when your hot pursuit had fizzled into boredom.'

'Why do you always do that?' he queried softly. The softness in his voice was deceptive, she could tell. It didn't match the steel-hard set of his jaw at all.

'Do what?' she countered sweetly. 'Fidget with my hair the way you used to tell me not to?'

'No. Put yourself down. Pretend to be a brainless doll, when you know damn well you've got a high IQ and unlimited potential.'

'Spare me the patronising vote of confidence!' she snapped, taking another sip of ouzo before pushing it away across the table. Since the vicious virus had attacked her, and over the prolonged recovery period she'd been forced to endure, she'd treated alcohol with wary respect. Since she'd been ill it had tasted as if it were triple strength, the way it had when she'd been in the early stages of pregnancy and hadn't known what it was that was wreaking havoc with her hormone system. 'Excuse me,' she added tautly, pushing her chair back and standing up. 'I get tired early. I'm going to bed.'

'Becky…' As she walked away she was conscious of the suppressed anger emanating from Matt as he slammed money on the table and grated back his chair to follow her.

She briefly caught a glimpse of her tense face

reflected in the wing-mirror of a car parked near by. She'd gone white, the scattering of freckles on her nose standing out lividly. Her hazel-brown eyes looked huge in contrast—dark hollows above the high cheekbones that had won her modelling acclaim.

'Becky, wait.' The hand catching her bare arm jolted her into stillness. Matt's voice sounded rough with impatience, slightly unsteady with anger. Abruptly, he swung her round to face him, and they stared at each other, motionless among the groups of people passing along the quayside. She flexed her arm slightly and his fingers tightened, biting into the soft flesh until she caught her lip in her teeth and sucked in her breath.

'Don't walk away from me,' he grated as she tore her arm away resentfully.

'Don't give me orders,' she managed. Her voice was husky with emotion, unsteady with nerves. He was standing so close that she could feel his heat, smell the clean, musky scent of the soap he used. The pulse beating in the side of his throat betrayed his tension.

Their eyes locked for a long moment, and then she shivered as he moved his gaze slowly, deliberately down, impassively noting the slim column of her throat, the photogenic leanness of her shoulders and arms, the soft contrast of the vulnerable swell of her breasts at the V-neck of her T-shirt. She caught her breath. His eyes felt like bold male fingers, seeking and touching, claiming rights of possession which she'd long since denied. She was hot, suddenly. Hot and shaking with reaction.

'I'll walk you back.' His tone was curt, but with a buried huskiness. 'I assume you're staying with Sofie and Richard?'

'I can find the way back all on my own,' she pointed out acidly. But he fell into step beside her anyway. And to her intense fury he slung a casual arm across her shoulders, meeting her disbelieving glare with a mocking twist of his mouth. Having Matt walk beside her, towering five inches taller than her slender five feet nine, and feeling the arrogant weight of his arm round her shoulders, brought back such painful memories of the past that she felt choked.

In a split second it all came back: the way her heart had leaped with joy the very first time he'd touched her, that idiotic surge of excitement and shyness she'd felt when he'd first reached for her hand, gravely examined it, then kept it in his, linking his strong fingers through hers, their palms touching with an intimacy and a shivery sensuality she'd never dreamed could come from a simple meeting of hands...

Her throat was dry as sandpaper now as she remembered. Briefly she squeezed her eyes shut, angry at her short-sighted belief that she'd stopped caring about Matt Hawke. She'd escaped from his magnetic presence, she'd hidden from him for two years, but she hadn't got over him. Now he was here again, and she was in danger of falling apart all over again.

'Matt...' They were outside the dark green door of Sofie's and Richard's house.

'Yes?'

'Please...' He'd dropped his arm from her shoulders. She couldn't read his expression; it was too complex.

'Please, what?'

There was a gleam of sensual awareness in his eyes, which disturbed her more than she cared to admit, and there was a coolly dissecting light too, which made her blood boil with suppressed anger. And there was a trace of amusement, which completely baffled her. What was so damn funny? she wondered crossly.

She forced herself to lift her chin and meet his narrowed gaze without flinching.

'Please don't make this any more difficult than it has to be,' she managed, with commendable briskness.

'At the risk of resembling a parrot—' he grinned faintly '—make *what* more difficult than it has to be, Becky? Taking my *wife* to bed with me, maybe, for old times' sake? Is that what this is all about?'

The heat coursed through her like flames. Trembling violently, she forced herself to smile with clenched teeth.

'No, Matt,' she managed evenly. 'Agreeing to the terms of our divorce. *That*'s what this is all about!'

CHAPTER TWO

'OUR divorce?' Matt's face had hardened into that expression which she knew so well—that cynical, shuttered gaze, which blocked any chance of reading his feelings but hid the shrewd calculation going on behind the dark mask. 'Is that what you want, Becky? Divorce?'

'What do you think? I see no point in being… being legally tied to you any longer. I assumed that was why you'd come to Skopelos! Didn't you get my solicitor's letter?'

He slowly shook his head. The gleam in his eyes was icily probing. She shivered, and took a step towards the doorway. Cowardly or not, she hated Matt in this determined, overbearing mood. That was one reason why she'd put off the dreaded moment, drifted on from month to month in the limbo of separation.

'No. I didn't get a letter,' he confirmed musingly. She had the unnerving sensation that he was sifting mentally through the facts and options, with the quick-fire agility that had made his name as a company trouble-shooter. Someone had once told her that Matt Hawke had the gift of assimilating every aspect of a complicated deal within ten minutes of receiving the relevant files. It was a special gift that had put him top of the list of every international board of directors who needed a sharp mind to extricate them from their financial catastrophes.

She could imagine him now, coldly weighing up his financial liability in terms of a divorce settlement...

'I've been out of contact for a while,' he added calmly. 'But if divorce is what you want, divorce is what you'd better have, my darling.' His voice held a drawl of mockery.

Becky's blood seemed to stand still, then turn to a trickle of ice in her veins. Why was she so shattered? Had she expected him to *argue*? Bitter self-mockery crashed down on her head like an avalanche. What a pathetic little fool she was.

'Thanks,' she managed drily. 'And don't worry. With—with no children involved I'm not after your precious money. All I want is my freedom.'

'Have you found someone else?' Matt's veiled gaze was unsettling. Whatever she'd expected, it hadn't been this poker-faced mildness.

'That's none of your business.'

'But you've hardly been *faithful* this last two years, I'd guess?'

'Don't try and drag me down to your level.'

Matt expelled his breath abruptly, and caught hold

of her shoulders. She tensed to defend herself, but
before she could gather strength he'd pulled her
close, too close. She was crushed against him, bitterly aware of his rock-hard muscle in contrast to
her slender softness.

'My level? I've never been quite sure where that
is in your eyes,' he grated roughly, catching her chin
and jerking up her face. The dark gleam in his eyes
seemed to probe inside her head. 'But have you always been little Miss Perfect? What about Ted
Whiteman...?'

She caught her breath. Ted had been a partner in
the modelling agency she'd worked for. But the suggestion that she'd had anything more than a business
relationship with him was absurd.

'Matt, your arrogance never fails to—'

His crude epithet cut across her sentence. Then
his mouth covered hers as he ducked his head to
kiss her, and the rest of her words were abruptly
muffled in the back of her throat.

His lips felt firm and warm, firing her whole body
with reaction. Becky stiffened and struggled, and he
deepened the kiss. His tongue drove inside to fence
and tangle with hers. Suddenly she was shaking
from head to toe with desire, as well as anger.

With a possessive jerk Matt pressed her closer.
His mouth hardened on hers, devouring, explicit
with the demand for more. His splayed fingers on
her back moulded her ruthlessly against him. Her

breasts tingled with response, the nipples becoming tight crests against the wall of his chest. Her stomach hollowed, heated with need. It had been so long since she'd felt this way, the shock made her head swim…

Just as violently she was free. Breathing raggedly, she stared up at him. She swayed slightly and he caught her again, his fingers moving rhythmically against the bare flesh of her upper arms. His eyes had darkened to a smoky blue.

'Becky…we have to talk,' he murmured, almost wryly. Desire had roughened his voice. 'This is crazy…'

'You're right. It is crazy. I'm not interested in *talking*, and I'm not interested in going to bed with you either!'

'Since you want a divorce, I imagine not.' The sarcastic tilt of his dark eyebrows made her blush. 'But we need to talk. Damn it to hell, you walked out on me without a word. Don't you think you owe me some civilised discussion?'

'Isn't it usually the solicitors who discuss things from now on?' She cursed the huskiness in her voice.

Could he tell how he was affecting her? Her heart jerked in her chest. They'd been together as man and wife for only six months, and at least half of that had been spent apart while he jetted around the world on business, but she'd be naïve to think that he couldn't pick up on her body language. He might be selfish and preoccupied with his business interests but he could be acutely perceptive when he wanted to be.

'I don't see any solicitors here, do you?' he countered coolly. A shadow of a grin touched his mouth. 'Have dinner with me tomorrow, Becky.'

'Make it lunch,' she suggested coldly. 'Dinner has too many...connotations.'

He studied her flushed face for a few moments, his eyes narrowing.

'Is it me you don't trust? Or yourself?'

She didn't even trust herself to answer, she realised despairingly.

'Do we have lunch or not?' she snapped.

'I have to go Athens tomorrow,' he said slowly, 'but I'll be back in time for dinner.'

'*Business*, I suppose?' she suggested, sweetly sarcastic.

'Naturally. Does a leopard change his spots?' Matt's gaze was glinting dangerously.

'Never. OK, dinner.' She forced herself to sound coldy casual. With a quick shrug she moved away from his hold, pressing her hands together behind her back.

She'd be better off humouring him rather than putting up too much of a tell-tale fight. The more she protested, the more he'd sense her vulnerability. And anyway...it wasn't as if she was likely to succumb to his lethal charm all over again. If she felt tempted then she only had to cast her mind back to the outcome of their last attempt at a relationship…

'I'll book a table at the Old Mill for nine, shall I?' she said.

'Fine. I'll see you there.'

'And if you don't turn up, owing to unavoidable business commitments, I won't be the least bit surprised,' she added flippantly, finding the key to the front door and turning her back on him. 'It will be just like old times! Goodnight, Matt.'

She let herself in and shut the door in his face, and then crumpled against the safety of the inner door like a rag doll. It took a huge amount of willpower to force herself along the hall and into her ground-floor bedroom, drag off her clothes and get ready for bed. She'd felt exhausted before—before Matt had reappeared tonight and knocked out what was left of her resilience. She just hoped that her recovery this time wouldn't take as long as it had during those months in Africa, where she'd picked up the virus!

Dinner tomorrow night with Matt. Why had she agreed? Because he'd cornered her, she accepted miserably. Because he'd wielded his powerful personality at her like a weapon the way he always had…

Lying in bed, restless and hot, naked beneath the light cotton sheet, she flopped her arms above her head on the pillow and squeezed her eyes tight shut to try to erase Matt's image and deny the pain of the past. It didn't work; she only saw him more vividly, in more detail. How come he looked so good, so relaxed and fit and brimming with self-confidence, while she felt as if she'd been through hell these last two years?

She opened her eyes again in the darkness, and the white walls of the bedroom seemed to be imprinted with his picture, and the murmur of voices, the sound of footsteps passing on the narrow street outside, seemed to mock her with the memories she longed to discard...

She'd been just nineteen when they'd met. It had been early summer, and she'd been staying here in this very house in Skopelos Town, in this very room, taking a fortnight's holiday after a trip to the Greek Islands for a catalogue shoot, and occasionally helping Sofie and Richard at their restaurant—just the way she was now. Except she hadn't been the way she was now; she'd been bubbling with the sheer delight of her luck in part-time modelling and her life as a first-year psychology student at London University.

One day she'd been doing a Christmas holiday job as a waitress in a bistro in Camden Town, the next she'd been spotted by a stylist from the well-known Ted Whiteman Agency, and been whisked from obscurity and relative poverty into the well-paid world of fashion magazine shoots, catwalk work, beauty advertisements and even television commercials—all fitted in around lectures and seminars.

That summer, Matt Hawke had just completed an assignment with a shipping company based in Athens, and had then been invited to join two of the company directors for a week's sailing around the islands.

He'd brought them to meet Sofie and Richard at their Old Mill Restaurant on Skopelos, and Becky, her mind preoccupied with other things, had gone to clear their table and had tipped the remains of his sorrel soup into his lap.

'Lucky that was cold,' he drawled, tilting his chair back and enduring her distraught attempts to mop up the spill from his jeans with amusement tugging at the corners of his mouth. 'You'd better let me wipe it up, don't you think?'

She froze with the napkin in her hand, suddenly aware of the precise location of the spilled soup, and met his eyes for the first time. The brilliance of that wickedly confident blue gaze demolished what was left of her poise. She blushed beetroot.

'I'm really terribly sorry,' she managed weakly.

The grin widened. He lazily extended a hand in greeting.

'Matt Hawke. And you're Sofie's little sister Becky. You don't remember me, do you?'

'Matt Hawke...?' After a few seconds' blankness, memory stabbed back with total clarity, and she blushed even harder.

In jeans and a casual denim shirt, he looked very different from the man in formal top hat and tails whom she'd first met seven years before. But she recognised him. Pride, however, had made her wary of admitting it, since she'd once nursed a brief but major crush on him for a couple of months after her sister's wedding.

She pictured the occasion instantly—the steamy marquee on a rainy June Saturday in deepest Somerset, champagne and crowds of well-dressed guests, a deafening hubbub of conversation, the uncomfortable stiffness of her peach taffeta bridesmaid's dress, the in-between awkwardness of being twelve years old with a brace on her teeth, stick-straight brown hair and non-existent breasts that were refusing to develop like her friends', and a feeling of being extremely small and insignificant...

'Richard's best man,' he supplied helpfully, 'and you were the chief bridesmaid. Remember?'

She'd certainly been the oldest bridesmaid, but she hadn't felt as important as the title implied. Richard's father had married twice, and there'd been a bevy of tiny, ringleted little sisters, nieces and cousins on his side to steal the show in identical little peach dresses. She could recall the way they'd gravitated towards the tall dark best man, who'd teased and entertained them with effortless humour.

'Er—yes...I think I remember. Seven years is a long time, though. You must have a good memory for faces.'

'I saw a picture of you in my Sunday newspaper a couple of weeks ago.'

'You did?' She felt mesmerised by his sheer magnetism. The clasp of his hand was like a brand of fire on the smoothness of her palm.

'Modelling some kind of miracle bra which you definitely don't look as if you need,' he purred, with such a dance of humour in his eyes that she melted totally and burst out laughing, in spite of the pinkness of her cheeks. In contrast with her gaucheness at their last meeting, she had enough confidence by now to know that his remark wasn't meant as a criticism.

'I'm definitely better at modelling than being a waitress.'

'I won't argue with that...'

The two dark-eyed Greek men with him eyed her with undisguised appreciation, but it was Matt who held her attention, who seemed to suck her into some invisible vacuum where only his slitted blue gaze and his mocking smile seemed real.

The cool admiration in his eyes seemed to fizz through her veins like soda; seemed to render her thighs weak and her heartbeat irregular and her breathing decidedly erratic. Not even the assessing male inspection, moving with an arrogant glitter of curiosity over her slender body in her loose green ethnic-print sundress, could bring her down to earth in time to save her from her own stupidity...

After that, Matt elected to stay a few days longer on Skopelos, while his Greek companions sailed off back to the mainland. He found himself a luxury room at a hotel just around the bay, hired an open top Jeep, and engulfed Becky in the potent spell of his company.

For three days they drove to secluded coves, picnicked under the pine trees, swam in the clear-as-glass Aegean, walked in the cooler evenings up to tiny chapels and mysterious little shrines to long-dead saints, and ate feta cheese omelettes or Greek salads with local bread and white wine and ouzo in tiny tavernas tucked away amongst the hills.

Sofie wryly gave her a brief résumé of his meteoric career, and the gossip-column status of his love-life, and warned her not to take him seriously. He was only twenty-eight, but already he'd climbed from investment banking in New York to becoming financial director of a big international property group, with several other directorships where ruthless tactics were required; and he was reputed to have broken as many hearts as he'd broken up companies for profit.

But by the time she'd spent three days in his company, talking about anything and everything—from university life to opera, from sailing to rock music, from the intricacies of her psychology course to Matt's pragmatic quest for wealth and power—she could hardly contain her quivering need for him to touch her, kiss her, demonstrate physically what his eyes had been coolly telling her all along.

Shyness and inexperience made her agonisingly tense whenever his hand brushed her arm, or the heat from his thigh came too close to hers. But inside she was in molten chaos.

On the fourth night, Matt drove her back to Sofie's and Richard's house in Skopelos Town, and instead of calmly bidding her goodnight he turned in the driving-seat and inspected her for what seemed like an eternity, before slowly reaching out to slide his palm along the smoothness of her upper arm.

She was unable to breathe; her lungs had contracted, expelled all her breath and then stayed paralysed. Statue-like, but burning inside, she sat there while Matt caressed her arm, moved his hand higher to smooth the contour of her shoulder, her throat, the delicate line of her jaw, and the small plump lobe of her ear.

Had she imagined that his hand shook slightly? She was never sure if he'd found that exploration as emotion-charged as she had, or if her own heightened senses had blinded her to reality.

He slid his hand down, brushing lightly against the swell of her breast, to take her hand, examining it with a wry gleam in his eyes, linking his fingers with hers, pressing the warmth of his palm against hers in what felt like the most unbearable intimacy.

'Goodnight, Becky.' The deep voice sounded hoarser than normal. She trembled with longing.

'Matt, don't go.' She breathed it without knowing how she had the nerve. Her husky plea brought a split-second stillness, then a deep groan of laughter from Matt as he jerked her into his arms.

'God, you're too young,' he murmured thickly, releasing her hand to smooth his fingers all the way up to her face, cupping her hot cheeks, sending tingles of exhilaration and fear into every distant corner of her body. 'Sofie will strangle me...'

'It's nothing to do with Sofie,' she managed weakly, before his lips sought hers, and his tongue was in her mouth, and his hands were moving on her body with an abrupt, seeking hunger which catapulted her into panic-stricken desire. 'And anyway...since when was kissing a capital offence?' she finished up with shaky humour, when Matt allowed her to surface for air.

'Since it led to what I'd like to do with you right now, little Becky.' His voice shook with humour and raw desire.

'I'm hardly that little,' she reasoned unsteadily, meeting his lidded blue gaze with a wide-eyed hazel stare which told him everything he needed to know about her lack of experience, and her acute vulnerability.

'No, you're not, are you?' But he sounded preoccupied. Abruptly he saw her into the house, and the next morning Sofie told her that he'd gone.

The rest of her stay in Skopelos had been like a grey memory—bleak despite the Greek blue sky and the brilliant sunlight. And life had stayed that way until he'd appeared in the doorway of her Hampstead bedsit, eight weeks later, slightly haggard-looking despite a dusky tan, slightly under the influence of whisky, dark and devastatingly male and announcing that he couldn't stay away any longer...

Lying remembering, in the small white-walled bedroom in Sofie's house, in the warm darkness of the night, Becky shuddered in spite of the heat. She'd never forget that night...

She turned miserably on to her face and buried her head in her pillow, trying to make her mind go blank. There was a high-pitched drone somewhere in the room. With a jolt of realisation she sat up wearily and clicked on the light; she'd forgotten to plug in the electric mosquito repeller. The bedroom was humming with thirsty Greek mosquitos. That was all she needed to round off a great evening, she told herself bitterly.

Sleep now felt impossible. Jumping crossly out of bed, she found a long, floppy white T-shirt and black leggings, and thrust them on, pushing her bare feet into flat black loafers. She brushed her hair and caught it up in a pony-tail to cool her neck. Before she left the room, she plugged in the little blue machine, sprayed some mosquito repellant on herself, and cast a final glare back at the uninvited flying occupants of the room.

'Die!' she told them emphatically, and abandoned the muggy warmth of the house for the cool night outside. She let herself out quietly. Sofie and Richard had come back around an hour ago, and she knew they wouldn't appreciate being woken from their hard-earned sleep.

The early hours of the morning in Skopelos Town were magically calm and curiously unthreatening, despite the shadowy darkness of the narrow streets, the ancient cobbles and inky black alleys plunging off in all directions.

She emerged on to the waterfront and walked slowly down past the closed cafés beneath the plane trees. A bat swooped up towards the eaves of one of the tall buildings. An almost deafening shrill of crickets came from the pine-clad hills behind her. There was a blissfully refreshing breeze coming off the sea.

Was Matt's boat moored along here? She'd headed for the water without thinking. Now she found herself wondering uneasily which of the many shining white yachts he was sleeping in right now.

The Aegean glittered black and silver in the eerie moonlight. Boats at the quay rocked and creaked slightly, moving on the swell from the wake of some far-off ferry which was ploughing through the darkness towards the mainland.

There was the muffled, soft sound of a scuffed footstep somewhere behind her in the stillness. Becky felt the tiny hairs on her nape rise, and was furious with herself. This was Skopelos, not some inner-city slum. She needn't imagine the worst just because someone else was suffering from insomnia along with her...

Forcing herself to keep walking nonchalantly, she quickened her pace a fraction even so. Maybe strolling around in the dead of night wasn't such a good idea. Maybe she'd make a hasty retreat back to Sofie's and Richard's house, and count dead mosquitoes...

Someone was behind her. The footsteps were soft enough to be made by trainers, but the sound was unmistakable. It was no good, she had to glance over her shoulder.

A tall dark figure, definitely male, was prowling along, shadowing her. Her heart skipped a beat then began to thud harder. It was obviously just someone off one of the boats, having a night-time stroll. But out here alone, despite her earlier confidence, she felt acutely vulnerable…

If she walked even faster…? If she started to run…? Would he run after her? She had long legs, and at school she'd excelled at the one hundred metres sprint, but since she'd had the virus she'd lost a lot of energy.

Panic took over from logical reasoning. She half turned, glimpsed him gaining on her, and started to jog. So did he. Whatever her past prowess in the one hundred metres, her pursuer was clearly in a different league. He gained on her effortlessly. A few moments later, pure terror ripped through her as she felt a powerful hand take hold of her arm.

She struggled like a wildcat, threshing her arms to free herself, aiming blind blows towards her assailant until a deep, husky voice said reprovingly. 'Cool down. Are you trying to get yourself raped or murdered, Becky?'

Spinning round, she faced Matt breathlessly, feeling very silly and extremely angry. Relief and annoyance mingled confusingly.

'It's *you*!' she hissed unsteadily, furiously aware that he was perfectly in control while she was gasping for breath, sweating all over and felt weak at the knees. 'Did you think giving me a heart attack was cheaper than divorce?'

'That thought hadn't occurred to me.' His grin

was a cruel slash of white in the dark. 'I was sitting on deck, drinking a middle-of-the-nightcap, and saw you wandering along on your own. I felt honour-bound to follow to keep an eye on you.'

'Well, thank you so much! How have I managed to survive these last two years without you to watch over me?'

Her bitter sarcasm provoked no visible response.

'Couldn't you sleep?' he queried, his voice a fraction quieter.

'Evidently not. Which apparently makes two of us.'

He slowly inclined his head. He looked thoughtful as he scanned her sudden pallor, noted the painful way she dragged air into her lungs.

'What's wrong, Becky? You look ill.'

'I felt perfectly all right until you came along,' she began tautly, but all the time she was aware of a disturbing lack of balance. The quayside, the dark sea, the rows of faintly tinkling masts had begun to pitch and slant at a nauseating angle. 'To tell the truth…I'm afraid I don't feel quite right…'

Her words dried up. To her horror she felt herself beginning to collapse. Before she could crumple to the stone pavement, Matt bent with swift decisiveness to gather her into his arms.

With her forehead heavy against his shoulder, one strong arm under her knees and the other firmly clasping her round the waist, he carried her, like a pirate with his prize, back to his boat…

CHAPTER THREE

'WHATEVER went wrong in our marriage, Becky—'
Matt sounded coolly derisive as he deposited her on
a bench seat in the saloon '—our separation doesn't
seem to have agreed with you.'

'Don't be so *condescending*.'

'You look bloody awful,' he said flatly. Sitting
down opposite her, he scanned her drawn face and
shadowed eyes, his own expression bland.

'Thanks for the compliment,' she managed
tightly. She was very angry with him, but the truth
was that she *felt* awful. Running like that, panicking
and getting the adrenalin surging crazily, had triggered a weak, exhausted sensation that made her feel
vulnerable.

She'd felt like this, off and on, ever since she'd
been sent home from Africa. She was her own worst
enemy, Sofie had declared. She should rest and relax
more. But the trouble with resting and relaxing was
that it gave her brain a chance to think too much.
Thinking…thinking about the past, about the disas-
ter of her relationship with Matt—that was her real
enemy…

'I'm fine. Well on the road to recovery,' she added quietly. Matt seemed to be considering this declaration. She felt his blue gaze move over her, from her hair in its casual pony-tail to her long baggy T-shirt and leggings. She winced slightly under the probing scrutiny and belatedly recalled that she was wearing no underwear; her hasty exit from her room had been too bleary-eyed, too spur-of-the-moment.

She hugged her arms protectively over the high swell of her breasts. In spite of her light-headed tiredness, she was very aware of him. So what was new? she thought nervously. Hadn't she always been? She couldn't recall a time when she hadn't been aware of Matt Hawke.

Sitting opposite her now, on the quietly creaking yacht, he was darkly disturbing. It was almost impossible to believe that she'd actually been married to him—was still married to him—that they'd spent six months being man and wife. He was like a stranger. Cool, cagey, exuding just the faintest air of danger, the way he always had…

'Sofie must be half-witted, letting you wait at tables at the Old Mill in this state.'

'Will you stop fussing?' she stormed, abruptly furious. '*I* chose to help Sofie and Richard. They're having financial problems this summer—they deserve any extra help they can get!'

She bit her lip in remorse. He'd goaded her into

divulging a confidence which she'd had no right to divulge. It was too late now.

Matt rubbed his chin slowly. The slight rasp of stubble as he stroked his thumb thoughtfully across his jaw was a very masculine sound. The narrowed gaze was laser-sharp as he watched her.

'What's their problem?'

There was no point in lying, Becky reasoned miserably. The secret was already out.

'The—the lease on the restaurant premises is about to expire. They either have to buy the whole thing outright, or get out. After they've built up such a fantastic trade. It's so unfair...'

'When's the deadline?'

'The end of the season.' Unable to stop herself, she felt a huge yawn welling up. Exhaustion was coming over her in waves, too powerful to fight.

'How does it help their finances if you run yourself into the ground clearing a few plates?'

'Have you ever heard of *moral* support?' she shot back witheringly. He certainly hadn't. If he had, she wouldn't have suffered that terrible loneliness after her miscarriage. She wouldn't have felt abandoned, unwanted, no longer a *necessary* accessory to Matt Hawke's high-powered life...

'You're shattered,' Matt stated expressionlessly. 'You need a course of early nights and healthy living.'

'Since when did you become a health freak?' Her

glare was somewhat diminished by having to struggle to keep her eyelids open. 'You're the original jet-lagged, stressed-out businessman, aren't you?'

Matt ignored her. 'You can bunk down here for the rest of the night.'

'*No!*'

'Why not?' He was hauling her to her feet, steering her through into a cabin towards the bows of the yacht. 'You're in no state to walk back to Richard's and Sofie's house. If it's wicked seduction that's bothering you, you're safe tonight. Sex with the walking dead is not my scene.' The caustic mockery caught her on the raw.

'You're such a gentleman,' she managed bitterly. 'Always ready with the chivalrous quip.'

'The heads are en-suite,' he drawled, flicking open a mahogany-panelled door to reveal a neat little bathroom equipped with everything, right down to gold taps. 'Are you going to be sensible, or do I have to lock you in?'

'Matt…'

'OK, don't look so panicky.' He shot her a wry glance as she sat there on the edge of the double bunk, trembling with frustration and exhaustion. 'Just get some sleep. That's an order!'

It was a measure of her intense tiredness that she allowed this last piece of arrogance to go unanswered. She keeled over on to the bunk as he left her, and blackness descended with such speed that she was deeply asleep, bordering on comatose, almost before her head hit the pillow.

She woke to an unnerving disorientation. Nothing seemed familiar, or even identifiable. She'd been dreaming that she was flying, weightless and floating high in the sky. There'd been a rush of air, streaming past her face, swishing like water. Now, lying flat on her back, still feeling weightless, she tried to work out where she was—where the curious dream ended and reality began.

Memory came back in a rush. She'd slept the night on Matt's yacht. And this morning the sun was slanting in through the smoked glass roof-light, and the boat was dipping and rocking on a strong swell—presumably the wake of a very large ferry indeed or, alternatively, they were moving!

Catapulting herself off the bunk, she dragged off the pony-tail holder and raked her trembling fingers through her hair as she staggered to the en-suite heads and splashed copious cold water over her face. Then, still feeling rumpled and grubby in her slept-in clothes, she flung open the cabin door.

Through the length of the saloon, with its mahogany table and neat navy blue tweed benches, she could see the cockpit ladder, and through the hatch she could see Matt, calmly at the helm. In deck-shoes, denims and a collarless white linen shirt, the wind ruffling his wavy black hair, he looked relaxed, unconcerned and totally in control, coolly squinting ahead through narrowed eyes.

Disbelief flooded her. How dared he…? How *dared* he? Almost blind with fury, she stumbled the length of the saloon, banging her thigh on the edge of the table and gritting her teeth as the pain fanned her anger. She marched through the compact galley and erupted up the steps and out of the open hatch to confront him. Seeing him glance down at her and then continue nonchalantly to man the helm made her catch her breath in rage.

'What are you doing?' she managed. It took every last shred of self-control for her to stop herself screaming at him like a banshee.

'Sailing.'

'I can see that.' She climbed out into the cockpit, glaring at him impotently. The wind caught her hair, tossing it round her face in a hazel-brown curtain. She scooped it away from her eyes impatiently, staring rather wildly around her. They were far out to sea, although misty humps of land could be seen vaguely in the distance in several directions. She tried for calm sarcasm.

'Maybe you forgot I was on board?'

'Nope.'

Matt's face was a mask, blandly unreadable. But something about the set of his jaw made her heart plummet. She recognised that look—sheer, ruthless bloodymindedness.

'Then maybe you'd like to turn this boat around and take me back to Skopelos?'

He shook his head, his mouth twisting wryly.

'*Matt*, this isn't funny!'

'It's not a joke.'

'Where are we going?'

'I fancied a spot of island-hopping.'

Her eyes widened to dark gold circles in her pale face.

'What about *me*? I don't happen to fancy "a spot of island hopping" in case you're interested, and you've got the biggest nerve—setting sail without even *asking* me if I fancied "a spot of island hopping"!'

'Becky, shut up and get us some breakfast, will you?'

'I will not shut up! And get your own damn breakfast! And if this boat isn't turned around and heading back to Skopelos by the time I've had a shower, I'll...'

'You'll what?' He grinned remorselessly. It struck her that Matt was thoroughly enjoying being as arrogant and overbearing as possible. Rage mingled with the beginnings of despair.

'I'll turn it round myself!' she tossed at him bitterly, turning to march back down to her cabin on legs which felt shaky with emotion.

A wild threat, she acknowledged chokingly as she flung off her clothes and squeezed herself into the small shower. Hanging on a rope from the shower attachment was a bottle of green shower-gel which could double as shampoo. It smelled soothingly of lemon and wild herbs—the kind of heady scent which came from the hillsides of sunbaked Greek islands. She refused to be soothed; outrage was a powerful emotion, and right now she was so outraged she felt that she might burst with it.

She used the gel copiously to wash herself and her hair as squeaky-clean as possible. She found clean, fluffy white towels in a small cupboard above the washbasin, and scrubbed herself dry with therapeutic violence. A tube of spearmint toothpaste was lodged into a neat holder with Matt's toothbrush; she spread an inch on her finger and cleaned her teeth, seething inwardly.

She'd been *kidnapped*, she thought mutinously. It was as simple as that. Kidnapping was definitely a crime, wasn't it? Could she have him arrested? Daydreams of seeing Matt marched away in handcuffs by some mean-looking Greek police officers afforded her short-lived consolation. Knowing Matt, he'd have the necessary contact in high places and be free in seconds...

As she donned her basic wardrobe again and prepared to emerge she became aware of a change in the rhythm of the boat. The dipping and swishing had faded. They'd slowed, stopped. Was he relenting? Preparing to turn back?

With as much dignity as she could muster, she stalked out to investigate. On deck, frigidly avoiding Matt's eyes, she saw that they'd dropped anchor in a deserted cove. A low, rocky-looking island lay a few hundred yards from the boat. Wild olive and low-growing scrub appeared to be the only vegetation. A waft of wild thyme blew towards her as she stared across the crystal blue water.

'A good spot for breakfast,' Matt explained calmly. He'd ducked below to the galley, and was rummaging in the small fridge. 'You didn't seem keen on cooking, so I'll rustle something up. Are you hungry? I'm ravenous.'

'I couldn't eat a thing. Matt, this has gone far enough. Take me *back*! *Now*!'

He straightened up, and met her burning glare with a cool, lidded gaze. The glitter in his blue eyes was mocking but determined.

'No way. Look on this as enforced therapy, Becky. You're forsaking civilisation until you gain half a stone and get some colour in your cheeks.'

'*What*? Are you demented? You can't kidnap me and—and force-feed me!' She found she was almost laughing at the farcical situation. Matt Hawke—professing concern for her health and well-being? Appointing himself her keeper for the duration of her recovery? She must be asleep, and dreaming. Or having a nightmare more likely.

'The force-feeding could be a problem,' he admitted drily. There was a wicked quirk of humour at the corner of his mouth. 'But the kidnapping was easy. Accept it gracefully, Becky.'

'I'd rather *die*!' she spat, incensed beyond logic. 'You wait until my solicitors hear about this…!'

'Divorce is a demanding business,' Matt pointed out, tossing four rashers of bacon into a hot frying-pan and pushing them around casually with a wooden spatula. The aroma which immediately invaded the air was so mouth-watering that she almost cried out; she hadn't realised how hungry she was until now.

'What are you talking about?'

'You need to be fit to cope with it,' he finished up, his mouth twisting. 'You're not even fit enough to boil an egg.'

She sat down suddenly on the bottom cockpit step, and stared at him in mounting panic. He was serious. He really meant this. Matt Hawke, her soon-to-be-ex-husband, was on some kind of crazy power-trip, and he'd kidnapped her in his boat and he was refusing to take her back to civilisation.

'Just a minute, didn't you say you had to go to Athens today on business?' she tried, attempting to inject some sweet reason into her voice. Maybe he'd really flipped. Maybe he was having some kind of off-beat mental breakdown. The wild possibilities crowded into her mind as she stared at him.

'I've postponed it. One egg or two?'

She sunk her face into her hands, and closed her eyes despairingly.

'None,' she told him, her voice muffled against her chest. When she lifted her head again, she saw that he'd broken four eggs into the pan.

'Matt...' She tried again. 'Sofie will be really worried about me.'

'That's taken care of. I radioed a message; the harbour-master will telephone her.'

'How efficient. So how long are you planning on playing this game?'

'As long as it takes. Do you want tea or coffee?'

'I always drink tea with my breakfast. Not that I'd expect you to remember!'

'Milk and sugar?' He was deliberately provoking her, but she couldn't help the surge of indignation.

'I *still* take milk and no sugar, Matt,' she retorted with elaborate politeness.

He'd switched off the heat and was expertly flicking the fried breakfast on to two plates. As he carried them over to the table he glanced across at her, his eyes veiled.

'If you walk out on someone and make no contact for two years, Becky, you don't expect them to remember how you take your tea in the mornings.'

She stood up and stared at him warily. The silence was suddenly redolent with unspoken words, buried grievances. It stretched between them like a taut wire.

'The past is over,' she said finally. She watched him gather knives and forks from a drawer, sit down casually and begin to eat the appetising-looking bacon and eggs. 'There's no point dragging it all up again now.'

'Maybe not.' He shrugged coolly. 'Come and have breakfast.'

She toyed with the option of tipping it over his arrogant head, but hunger conquered pride. She wasn't just hungry, she acknowledged reluctantly, walking slowly to the table; she felt as if she hadn't eaten for a week. Abruptly she sat down opposite him at the narrow table, and began to eat her first meal with Matt for two years.

'So, tell me what you've been doing,' he suggested with a cool drawl, after they'd eaten in tense silence for a while. 'Where've you been hiding from me?'

'Hiding from you?' She'd nearly finished the food. She had to concede that Matt had surprised her; she'd never known him cook anything before. What was more, it tasted good.

She stared at him now, her eyes widening in disbelief. 'Don't start trying to tell me that you cared *where* I'd gone, or whether I was hiding from you or not. I'm surprised that you even noticed I'd left. I didn't need to hide from you; I only saw you a handful of times in the whole time we were married!'

'That…' he paused to finish the meal, taking healthy relish in the food before pushing his knife and fork neatly together '…is a slight exaggeration, Becky.'

'No, it's not! We had our crazy, whirlwind love-affair in between your trips to New York, Hong Kong and—and the Planet Zog for all I know… I got pregnant, we got married. I lost the baby, and—hey presto!—the famous vanishing husband!'

A glimmer of emotion lurked in his eyes, but she couldn't tell what he was thinking. That was what she was finding so unnerving about Matt, she realised with a jolt. She had no idea what his motives were. If she'd ever understood anything about the man she'd married in haste he was uncharted territory to her now.

'I didn't vanish; I travelled abroad on business,' he pointed out calmly. 'You could have come with me.'

'Oh, yes, so I could. And played gooseberry to you and Su-Lin!'

Standing up abruptly, he took their plates to the small sink and brought cups of tea back to the table.

'Instead you chose to stay at home and play the neurotic abandoned wife?'

She stared at him, white-faced.

'That's not true…'

'Isn't it?' The dark blue eyes were slitted to a ruthless glitter. 'Didn't you prefer to stay in

Hampstead bewailing the loss of your modelling career with Ted Whiteman?'

'That's not fair.' Her voice was a husky whisper. 'You know that's not fair, Matt!' She was shaking. Jumping to her feet, she stared at him, fists clenched, bitterness and hatred all mixed up with confusion and despair.

'I know what you're trying to do,' she said unsteadily, with mounting fury. 'You're trying to switch the blame for our break-up on to me. Is that some neat legal technicality? Does it mean that you don't have to fork out so much in the divorce settlement or something? Tell me, Matt. I don't know much about the legalities of divorce, but I'm sure you do! You'll have consulted the top international divorce lawyers, obtained the very best advice, of course—'

He'd rounded the table and grabbed her by the shoulders as the torrent of words poured on. He gave her a short, brutal shake.

'Stop it, Becky! You're getting hysterical!'

'Hysterical? How convenient that men always use that word when a woman is telling them things they don't want to hear. Let *go* of me!'

She was writhing and struggling to free herself from his grasp. Matt's short epithet was lamentably crude. With a jerk, he imprisoned her in his arms, dropping his head determinedly. He kissed her hard, with punishing demand, on the mouth.

The contact felt like a lightning strike—searing and scorching. Her indignation made her stiffen like a statue in his arms. He deepened the kiss, intensifying the onslaught. Response tore through her, its flames flickering inside her, unexpected and humiliating. How could he provoke her to this? So fast? With such arrogant ease?

The feel of his strong hands, thrusting hungrily beneath her T-shirt, finding the smoothness of her bare midriff, lingering just beneath the high mound of her breasts, brought goose-bumps springing to the surface of her body. Her brain whirred furiously. It didn't appear to connect any longer with her heart— or her baser instincts. Whatever part of her it was that controlled those was leaping ecstatically in the flames, abandoning itself with shameless enthusiasm to the physical conflagration Matt had always promised, always supplied...

'Matt, this won't solve anything,' she managed hoarsely. But she shuddered against him, her hands beginning to push at his shoulders then curling involuntarily around the hard muscle beneath her fingers.

He lifted his head to gaze at her flushed face and parted lips. His reply was a husky grunt of amusement stirred thickly with desire. As he wrenched her hips closer to his she felt the unmistakable threat of his arousal, hard and powerful against her stomach. Spreading his muscular thighs, he pulled her even closer, moulding her between his legs, watching her over-bright eyes dilate in alarmed, mute reaction.

'Maybe not,' he agreed raspingly, 'but it beats the hell out of arguing.'

'Matt—'

He covered her mouth again, and this time the force of his desire broke over her. It overwhelmed her, like a tidal wave engulfing a lone protester. In spite of herself, beside herself, she was caught up and simultaneously dragged down with him. The inundation stopped conscious thought, reduced her to pliant jelly.

He wrenched the T-shirt up and over her head. Breathing deeply, she shivered convulsively under the burning blue gaze trained intently on the soft, female curves revealed to his view.

'Too thin but still beautiful,' he breathed roughly. 'Still the most desirable body I've ever seen, Becky.'

He was shaking too, she dimly realised. But surely his was a controlled emotion, because he was in charge and he knew it. Resentment, hurt and furious pride didn't stop her traitorous body from crumpling at the knees as he pulled her urgently down to the saloon floor. All she could think about was the clean male smell of him, the feel of his lean body against her, the remembered weight and muscularity of his limbs.

Matt Hawke was six feet one of forceful male

strength. The ruthless streak that won him business deals had a lot in common with the merciless inevitability of his lovemaking. He pinned her there with lethal decisiveness while his open mouth moved over her breasts, taking first one tight peach-pink nipple then the other, arousing her with his lips and his teeth until she was crying out helplessly, hardly aware of herself.

There was a hot gleam of anger as he gazed down at her. Anger? Or revenge? Through the mists of desire she battled to make sense of it. He moved to tug impatiently at the waistband of her leggings. The stretchy black material came down easily, exposing the bare, silky plane of her stomach, the vulnerable hollow of her groin, the beginning of the V of dark curls at the junction of her legs.

'My God—' his voice was suffused with raw hunger as he breathed the words against her hair '—I've spent the last two years wanting to feel you in my arms like this, Mrs Hawke...'

His softly dangerous tone snapped her back to her senses. As he levered an assertive knee between her legs, her sense of self-preservation rushed back to save her. What was wrong with her? Hadn't she spent the last two years vowing never, ever to let Matt take control of her again in this way?

Just in time she began to fight, to protect herself fiercely from the emotional suicide of giving herself to Matt. In spite of the hot ache of need in her stomach, the shameful tingling in her breasts, she managed to freeze, to push him violently away.

'Stop it, Matt!' Her warning held as much firmness as she could muster, and a very real tremble of fear. Matt was strong. Was he unprincipled enough just to carry on, take what he wanted, humiliate her to punish her for some imagined wrong...?

'Stop?' he mocked hoarsely, freeing her to a degree. 'Is that what you really want?

'Yes!'

'OK.' Slowly, with lidded eyes, he withdrew from her. She wasn't sure if she was more relieved or shocked when she felt his weight lifted and realised that she was free. 'If you really want me to stop...'

'I do,' she choked tearfully. Why was she crying? The hot tears stung, filling her throat.

'Before I do...' He slid his hand down with blatant intimacy to cup the melting heat of her sex, inside the stretchy leggings. She caught her breath on a sharp hiss of outrage as he discovered the telltale feminine slickness there, delved with brief, devastating boldness into the tight silken sheath, then pulled back with a sensuous stroke of clever male fingers, touching every secret place on his slow retreat.

'You *bastard*,' she said, quivering hotly. She was rewarded by a grim flash of a smile—the infuriating smile of a marauding bandit, biding his time.

'You're my legally wedded wife,' he reminded

her cynically, his voice still thick with desire, his blue gaze devastatingly sensual as he watched her scarlet face. 'And be honest, Mrs Hawke, you didn't want me to stop.'

Only the galling knowledge that she would probably come off worse stopped her from physically lashing out at him.

'If I ever had a second's doubt about the wisdom of leaving you, it just vanished!' she flung at him tightly. 'You haven't got a shred of chivalry in you! You use people. You can't resist the urge to win at any cost! Well, here's one you're going to lose, Matthew Hawke! If you think I'm *ever* going to meekly give in again to your *expert* charms, dream on!'

CHAPTER FOUR

'As I see it,' Matt said lazily, from his reclined position on the sun-drenched deck, 'we can play this in one of two ways: fight like cat and dog, or try being grown-up and civil to each other.'

'You've conveniently overlooked the third option,' she reminded him icily. 'You can sail this wretched boat back to Skopelos, leave me alone and get on with your usual jet-setting!'

She was sitting tensely at the other end of the deck, gazing with furious longing at the inviting sparkle of the Aegean lapping peacefully around the boat. Not only was she a prisoner on Matt's boat, she had only her T-shirt and leggings to wear. And stripping naked to dive into the sea was unthinkable with Matt's brooding presence watching her like a hawk.

There'd been a brief lull in hostilities while she'd marched to her cabin and simmered with frustration and outrage on the bunk. But the heat of the boat as the sun had climbed in the sky, and her mounting feeling that she was childishly sulking in her tent, had forced her out to face him again.

She'd told Matt yesterday that she'd matured since their break-up; she'd better prove it. She was still smarting with humiliation at his treatment of her, but if all else failed, there was the old saying 'Don't get mad, get even'. Maybe it wasn't such a smart move to show him how furious she was. Maybe she'd gain more satisfaction by biding her time, waiting for an appropriate moment to strike back...

'I haven't done much jet-setting recently,' he said lightly. Sprawling flat out, he linked his hands lazily behind his head. He'd slid on a pair of dark glasses; the added shield made his expression totally impenetrable.

'No? OK, you've taken a few weeks off to do some sailing,' she countered sarcastically, 'but you were still talking about going to Athens on business!'

'I didn't say I'd turned into a couch potato,' he murmured blandly.

'Quite. To be a couch potato you need to know what a couch is,' she taunted. 'Something people put in their homes to relax on together occasionally, in front of a cosy fire.'

'Are you saying that's why you walked out on me, Becky?' He lifted his head, his gaze directed at her from behind the sunglasses, 'Because we didn't sit holding hands watching soap operas often enough?'

She stood up restlessly. Keeping the lid on her anger was going to be a superhuman achievement, she realised bleakly. But flying into rages was simply playing into his hands. He must be enjoying every chauvinistic, domineering second of this…

She went to lean on the brass rail surrounding the deck.

'Frankly, Matt,' she said quietly, 'I think you must have been watching too *many* soap operas! This situation is straight from the script of a very *bad* soap opera! God knows what you hope to gain, but—'

'Time,' he said softly. 'That's what I hope to gain.'

She stiffened, turning slowly to stare at him. Her throat felt drier.

'"Time"? What do you mean, "time"?' she demanded coldly, 'Time for what?'

'Time to see you looking less like a refugee from a concentration camp.' The cool retort was expressionless. 'I told you, I'm worried about you.'

It was hopeless, she acknowledged, pushing her hands rather wildly through her hair and then dropping them despairingly at her sides.

'If you keep me on this boat much longer, I promise you I'm likely to lose even more weight,' she managed finally, keeping her voice cool and reasonable. 'And…and I'll probably succumb to half a dozen stress-related diseases! That's if I don't die of sheer boredom first. Or get eaten by sharks when I dive overboard to escape.'

'There are no man-eating sharks in the Aegean sea. And I think it's time to move on,' Matt announced, levering himself up in one fluid, muscular movement. He jumped easily down to join her, and cast her a cool grin as he ducked below. 'I think I'll change into shorts; it's getting hot.'

'That's another thing,' she called after him, through clenched teeth, 'what the hell am I supposed to *wear*? All I've got is the clothes I'm standing in!'

He reappeared at the hatch, his half-smile guaranteed to provoke.

'And very fetching you look in them, Mrs Hawke.'

'*Matt*! Seriously!'

'Seriously, I've probably got something suitable. A female who joined me for a while left some stuff behind; I'll take a look.'

Speechless, she watched him vanish below again. He was unbelievable. His arrogance, his insensitivity, appeared boundless. Almost paralysed with resentment, she waited until she had control of her reaction, gripping the handrail until her knuckles went white. Then she marched stiffly down to find him.

'Here we are.' He was reappearing from his cabin, nonchalantly clutching a handful of clothes, and wearing none himself.

Dragging a shaking breath into her lungs, she gazed at him. Anger over his cavalier suggestion of lending her another woman's clothes was mingled with the devastating experience of seeing Matt totally naked. Heat flooded her face, and she cursed her own gullibility. They were *married*, she had to remind herself. So what could be so disturbing about the mere sight of those tanned lean contours?

She couldn't tear her eyes away from the power of the muscled thighs, the ripple of strength in the shoulders, the flat-ridged abdomen, the areas where coarse black hair grew lightly on his chest and arrowed downwards to the overt masculinity in the denser hair below...

'I think she's about your size.' He was casually inspecting a beautiful tapestry-print swimsuit in soft shades of mauve, cream and green, a pair of bottle-green shorts, and a couple of sleeveless cream T-shirts. 'This is nice, don't you think?' He held out the swimsuit, his brilliant blue gaze coolly amused as he scanned her hot face. 'She bought it in Crete—'

'You expect me to wear the—the cast-off clothes of some woman you've had an affair with? You must be insane. And for heaven's sake put something on!'

Matt gazed at her affronted expression, and burst out laughing.

'Surely you can't be jealous?' he drawled. 'And

why are you blushing? We're still man and wife, sweetheart. Or have you turned into a prude?'

'I'm not a prude. And I'm not jealous about this other female; I'm…disgusted,' she bit out. 'Though why anything about you should surprise me, I can't imagine!'

'I'm getting pretty tired of hearing your sanctimonious, judgemental opinion of me,' Matt told her softly. The humour was fading from his dark face. 'But if it helps you to climb down off that proud pedestal you've put yourself on these belong to my sister Carrie.'

'Oh!' Her blush deepened.

'They're clean and they're relatively new,' he went on calmly, 'and she left them on the boat because she and her husband thought they might be joining me again later. Is that respectable enough for your delicate feelings, Becky?'

With a trembling hand, she took the clothes he was offering.

'If you'd said that in the first place…!' His closeness, the size and potent maleness of him were causing the blood to pound much too fast around her bloodstream.

'Since when have you believed anything I've said to you?'

Averting her eyes, she stalked back to her cabin, and shut the door firmly behind her. Her throat was dry, and she was hot and trembling all over, she realised furiously.

Matt had always had this knack of sending her pulse-rate soaring. But she'd hoped, fervently hoped, that she was over him. Some hope.

The knowledge terrified her. Holed up with him, in the claustrophobic confines of this yacht, it was going to take mammoth self-control to hide her re-actions to him. But she had to. She *had* to. She didn't dare let him get too close. She couldn't face going through all that pain again...

The swimsuit fitted perfectly—high at the leg, scooped deeply at the back, and rounded to a small zip-fastener over her breasts. The soft tapestry-effect jersey fabric was unusual—very foreign-looking. She checked her appearance in the long mirror on the back of the door, registering the cut and style with preoccupied approval.

Her mind was elsewhere, reluctantly jolted back in time. Carrie's name had triggered memories. Not particularly of Carrie, although she'd liked her very much when she'd met her. Bright and pretty, with dark hair and blue eyes, she'd been very like Matt—but the only time she'd ever met Matt's sister had been on her own wedding-day.

Images of that day—the day she and Matt had made their marriage vows in the small greystone church—now came crowding into her mind. She could see herself, walking radiantly up the aisle in her ivory silk dress. She could smell the faint, dusty scent of old wood, damp flagstones, incense and chrysanthemums and dahlias.

A surprisingly warm late October sun had been shining in through the big stained-glass window above the altar, throwing coloured patterns over the floor, over the congregation. She could see the reassuring breadth of Matt's shoulders as he stood at the front; could see vividly his dark, aquiline profile as he'd turned to watch her walk to his side.

She'd worn her hair down, a delicate wreath of white rosebuds and gypsophila on her head, and she'd been eight weeks pregnant...

That day had been the culmination of a passionate but unpredictable relationship lasting just under three months.

It had been in early August, that night when Matt had appeared on her doorstep. He'd just flown back from Hong Kong—straight back, she thought now bitterly, from the arms of Su-Lin. But at the time she'd had no way of knowing that Matt was unofficially engaged to the wealthy Chinese girl.

'It's the typhoon season over there,' was all he'd said about Hong Kong. 'I left the next round of business talks to a colleague. I'm sick of dodging tropical rainstorms. And I wanted to make love to you...'

The directness of his gaze, the kindling of dark desire in his eyes, had made her shiver all over with

response. He'd cut short her indignant protests, her
embarrassed apologies for the state of her bedsit,
sweeping her into his arms and elbowing his way
in, tipping the cascade of clothes and books from
the bed, and dropping down beside her on the green
and gold ethnic bedspread with such arrogant, com-
ical precision that they'd both dissolved into helpless laughter.

He kissed her and the laughter faded. He un-
dressed her slowly, and with each button opened,
each intimacy overcome, she melted like butter in a
naked flame. When he asked softly, 'Is it OK?' she
woefully misunderstood his meaning.

Finally, shaking all over with suppressed impatience, she watched him fling off the crumpled beige
linen suit, the white linen shirt, and let her eyes lin-
ger shyly on his glorious male strength just long
enough before he took her, forcefully—bordering on
violently—shuddering like a man possessed as he
claimed her virginity for himself.

'It's a long time since I was shocked by anything
to do with sex,' he drawled huskily, when the brief,
fierce battle was over, 'but I'm shocked.'

'Because I was a virgin?'

'Correct.' The deep voice held a wry trace of
mockery, but a rough tenderness too. 'You little
bird-brain—why did you say it was OK?'

'How was I to know what you meant?' She wriggled with outrage, but he held her still, imprisoning

her in such a way that all thought of escape, of vague disillusion with the much hyped act of love-making, faded into obscurity.

'I know your mother died years ago, but Sofie could have spelled out the facts of life to you before now?'

'I *know* the facts of life, you pig.'

'Hush, I'm just teasing. You're adorable, desirable, perfect in every way...' he murmured, his voice thickening again as he moved against her, smoothed clever hands along her arms, her legs, her breasts, her thighs, homing in on secret places in a way that sent her gasping for some fulfilment she could only vaguely imagine, something which seemed just out of reach but supremely, ecstatically desirable—until it was there for her in such volume and quality and intensity, rippling and erupting over her and inside her, that she nearly died of pleasure...

Becky caught a glimpse of herself now, standing motionless in front of the cabin door mirror. The person that she'd been in the past—the irresponsible, wildly optimistic romantic, certain of a rosy future, helplessly in love with the dark, forceful male who'd literally swept her off her feet and into his haphazard life—might just as well have died then.

She'd have been spared the agony of discovering that Matt didn't return her feelings, that the desire which had brought him pacing back to her door that night from his Hong Kong deals had been part of a peculiarly male pattern of behaviour—a need to conquer and possess, followed by a strong urge to move on to pastures new. Risk, excitement, the thrill of gambling and winning, the thirst for power: all those things, Matt Hawke craved like an addict.

Her biggest mistake had been letting him make love to her. Her second biggest mistake had been telling him, six weeks into their sporadic relationship, that on the first, uncontrollable night of their affair she'd conceived his child; that she was going to have his baby.

Instead of starting her second year at university that October she'd been drifting gullibly down the aisle, all studies abandoned, all modelling aspirations happily put on the back burner, lost in a romantic idyll, on her way to becoming Mrs Matthew Hawke and the biggest fool in the Western hemisphere—

'Becky?' Matt's voice cut through her trance of memories. There was a knock on the door. 'Are you OK in there?'

She compressed her lips, and reached for the shorts, stepping into them while she composed herself a little.

'Perfectly OK, thanks,' she managed coolly. 'What do you want?'

'Just checking you weren't flattened with seasickness,' he called back calmly. 'And, if not, do you want to come out and make some coffee?'

'Whatever you say. You're the *skipper.*' Her sweet sarcasm produced no reply. Pulling on one of the sleeveless cream T-shirts, she cautiously let herself out of the cabin and made her way carefully along to the galley.

Matt had returned to the helm. He'd put on some clothes, she noted with relief. Or, at least, he'd put on some shorts. Strong, darkly tanned legs emerged from rather battered-looking white denim bermudas. His upper half was still bare, glistening darkly bronze in the brilliant sunlight. She swallowed quickly, and looked away.

'Black or white?' she called flatly.

'Black with a dash; no sugar.' The wry amusement in his voice registered her small retaliation. 'And I wouldn't have expected you to remember something so trivial, Becky.'

She carried two mugs up on deck, and sat down as far from him as possible in the cockpit, blinking in the sun.

'There should be some spare sunglasses somewhere.' He glanced back, noticing her squint.

'Don't tell me—Carrie's?'

'Probably. Look on the plan table.'

She ducked below and found some, and thankfully put them on. Back in the cockpit, the milky coffee tasted warm and reviving, and the view across the churning water was frankly uplifting. She felt a small moment of calmness, like the eye in the centre of a hurricane. The air was pure, the distant islands indescribably beautiful. Matt was a bastard, but at least he was professing a degree of concern for her welfare. It was difficult not to relax a fraction—just a fraction...

'So tell me where you've been,' he invited nonchalantly, sitting down opposite her, having put the boat on automatic navigation. 'What have you been doing this last two years?'

'I went to Africa.' She took a shaky sip of her coffee, and watched the cool disbelief on his face.

'*Africa*?' he echoed blankly. 'What the hell were you doing in bloody Africa?'

'Working.'

'What kind of work?'

'*Voluntary* work. In a famine area. Helping people—children mainly. And babies...' She felt her throat tighten in warning as the emotional turmoil of her time there came back.

Matt was watching her, his eyes lidded. With the blue sky behind his head, his narrowed gaze was so brilliantly blue that his irises looked like slivers of lapis lazuli in the dark of his face.

'So *that*'s what you were up to,' he said expressionlessly. 'It's a far cry from modelling clothes.'

'Or doing a psychology degree?' She couldn't keep the defensiveness out of her voice.

'And that.'

There was a prolonged silence.

'Children sometimes get a raw deal in a lot of countries,' he said quietly. 'Why pick Africa when there must have been half a dozen to choose from?'

'Because the problems in Africa seemed to be the most dramatic, the most immediate.'

'Or because Africa seemed like the furthest you could get from me?'

She felt heat rush to her face. Anger stabbed back, but she suppressed it.

'What an ego,' she taunted evenly. 'You really believe that the entire world revolves around you, don't you?'

'Doesn't it?' His mock concern made her mouth twist into a reluctant smile in spite of her anger.

'Possibly not. And is there anything wrong with just wanting to do something to help people?'

'Without sounding like some earnest little do-gooder?' he queried with a cool grimace. 'I suppose not. But you seem to have conveniently forgotten something. You took off for darkest Africa to ''help people'' without so much as a forwarding address for the man you vowed to love, honour and obey six months previously in front of a congregation in church. You help some people, and kick a few others in the teeth. Is that the idea?'

Becky stared at him, slowly shaking her head.

'You should know,' she said unevenly. 'You're the expert.'

Matt's face hardened.

'They tell me that miscarriage can cause a personality change in women,' he said flatly. 'I married a girl with a sense of humour and a loving nature, and I ended up with a suspicious shrew.'

She felt every muscle in her body clench. His mention of losing the baby, clinical and dispassionate, choked her with bitter memories. That was typical of his reaction to the tragedy right from the start—calmly uncaring, unable to empathise with her in any way. She'd never felt so alone as in those bleak days after her miscarriage.

'Matt, I don't want to talk about this.' She stared at the turquoise sea where it shallowed towards a small island, keeping her gaze away from Matt's probing stare.

'I realise that. Why else would you vanish to the Dark Continent for two years without so much as a postcard?' There was a trace of cool mockery in his voice.

'To regain my self-esteem,' she told him, as calmly as she could.

'Which I, presumably, had trodden beneath my callous, uncaring feet?'

'You said it.' She was gripping her coffee-mug so hard that her fingers ached.

Matt stood up suddenly, unravelling his full, muscular height with lazy purposefulness. He came across to remove the mug from her stiff fingers. Grasping her arms, he pulled her up to stand in front of him. Rigid with denial, she strained to pull away. It was a waste of time, of course, she should know better by now, she told herself angrily. She was snared by his grip, and jerked closer. The space between their bodies narrowed to an agonising half-inch, which seemed to heat abruptly to steaming-point.

'Tell me one thing,' he bit out softly. 'Why didn't you *tell* me you were leaving? Why did you just disappear without a word, without even a god-damned note? Did you think I was made of steel, for God's sake? Didn't you realise that I'd be going out of my mind with worry?'

'Matt, you're hurting me...'

'Not half as much as you hurt me, Becky!'

Her head was spinning as she gazed up at him.

'Your pride, maybe?'

'So you think I've got no feelings?' he ground out. The ruthless anger in his face, the set of his jaw, the sudden blaze of fury in his eyes, were frightening and confusing. She'd started to tremble, she realised to her annoyance.

'What are you saying? That you might not have wanted me, but you'd have preferred no one else to have me either?'

'But other people did have you, didn't they,

Becky?' The rough shake he gave her went almost
unnoticed as blind anger consumed her. 'People like
Ted Whiteman? He was round at the house in
Hampstead so often that his mail was redirected,
wasn't it?'

'Don't be so ridiculous!'

'Kind, sympathetic Ted, with a shoulder to cry on
while your cruel bastard of a husband went to bed
with other women in Hong Kong?'

The relentless, icy mockery slashed her like a
knife-attack. She flinched as if he'd really cut her.

'Stop it…*stop* it!'

With a ragged groan, Matt seemed to get a hold
on his anger. Gathering her to him, he crushed her
hard against his chest. A shudder went through him.
He dropped his face to the top of her head.

'Hell, I'm sorry.'

'No, you're not.' Her voice was muffled against
the disturbing, hard warmth of his body.

'Becky.' Slowly, he stepped away from her, dropping his hands from her. His eyes were shuttered,
but there was a haggard look about his expression
despite the mocking twist of his lips. 'Becky… The
outcome may still be divorce, but we owe each other
a fair hearing. So far, all I've got to go on is what
Sofie told me, when I was tearing round trying to
find you.'

'I don't owe you anything!'

His gaze grew bleaker. 'Like hell you don't! It

was my baby too, you know! Do you think I wasn't grieving as well? Or don't *fathers* have feelings either?'

She stared at him. Her throat had dried. She moistened her lips, suddenly feeling crazily out of her depth. What was Matt trying to do? What was he hoping to achieve by this sudden pretence at having finer feelings?

'Matt,' she began carefully, taking a wary step back from him, 'when I had the miscarriage, you spent one night at home with me, then you caught a plane from Heathrow to New York, and from New York to Hong Kong, where you promptly took up again with the girl you were supposed to marry before I got pregnant and messed up your life for you! There were photos of you together in the gossip pages. It was common knowledge. That's the truth. You know it is.'

'Is there any point in my denying it?' The wry retort held such suppressed anger and the tautness of his jaw was so threatening that she shivered slightly. Lifting her chin to stop her anxiety showing, she glared at him.

'Hardly! This…this belated plan of yours somehow to give each other ''a fair hearing'' is just about as arrogant and—and pigheaded as possible! So why can't you stop harassing me like this and admit that our marriage was a mistake? Just turn round, and sail back to Skopelos, and call it a day?'

'Because I suspect that there are hidden depths in the wreckage of our relationship.' Was there just the faintest trace of menace in his mocking tone? 'Interesting angles I'm keen to explore before your solicitors step in and ruin everything.' Without warning, he caught hold of her again and tugged her with harsh determination into the circle of his arms. 'And one of them, my darling Mrs Hawke, is the way you tremble all over like this, when I kiss you...'

CHAPTER FIVE

HEAT flared so fast that Becky almost felt herself sizzle. It was that familiar, frightening spiral of response, making every nerve-end raw, melting her stomach and tingling through her breasts. But it was so confused with anger and resentment, so linked with humiliating surrender that she somehow found the strength to resist. She clamped down fast on her wayward emotions, freeing herself with a violent, determined push.

'Careful,' she breathed unevenly. 'You're not looking where we're going! I'm sure if it came down to mending our marriage or smashing up the boat, the boat would have priority.'

Matt levelled a dissecting gaze at her, then expelled his breath heavily. Wordlessly, he turned back to scan the horizon ahead of the moving boat. She stared at his powerful back, at the ripple of muscle as he moved, at the way his lean torso pulsed with his quickened breathing.

She was still inwardly reeling from the force of his kiss. Watching him now, she could see that he'd felt a similar flare of hunger. It hadn't been simulated, just to get his revenge on her for leaving him, he'd wanted her—physically. And now he was furious and frustrated, suppressing that frustration in his silent withdrawal. But she'd be naïve to feel flattered or warmed by the knowledge. Sexual desire was a mechanical reflex with men like Matt. If only she could treat it likewise, instead of fearing that her whole being would disintegrate if she risked that ultimate intimacy again…

'Is that what you think this is all about? Mending our marriage?' His voice, when he finally broke the taut silence, was expressionless. He didn't look around.

Her heart lurched painfully.

'We never really had a marriage,' she pointed out as calmly as she could, 'so there's nothing much to mend. If you want to know what I think, I think this is all about proving to yourself that you can have whatever you want until *you* choose to throw it away. It's getting your own back because you lost control of the situation when I walked out. It's about agreeing to a divorce on *your* terms. It's all about pride. And ego. Always having to be in control. Am I right?'

'Right now—' he sounded ominously calm '—it's about controlling the urge to throw you in the bloody sea.'

'Typical.' She fought down the wave of heat in her face. Clenching her hands into small fists of defence, she managed to taunt lightly, 'Threats. Anger. Why can't you take a rational view of things?'

'Stop being such a bitch, Becky,' he murmured, preoccupied with the automatic compass, his strong fingers lightly on the wheel. 'There's a sheltered cove around here. Perfect for a night-time mooring.'

'Perfect for you, maybe,' she shot back. 'When are you going to get it through your thick skull that I don't want to be here? That I don't want to be with *you*?'

'How about making the best of it by helping with the sailing?' His retort was cool, infuriatingly un-provoked.

'If you wanted willing crew, you should have picked a keen sailor. Anyway, I thought you'd been sailing around single-handed for most of these last few weeks?'

'Few months, in fact.' He was busily winding in one of the sails, the lean muscles in his arms glis-tening strongly as he worked.

'*Months*?' Had she heard him correctly? Hazel eyes widening, she stared at him questioningly.

'Yup. About three months, to be precise.'

She took a few moments to make sense of this.

'So…what about your *meteoric* career?' she man-aged at last. 'Your globe-trotting commitment to the work ethic?'

'If sarcasm is the only form of wit that you can

indulge in, don't bother.' He angled a dry grin over his shoulder.

'But seriously…' Curiosity overcame her annoyance. 'What's going on, Matt?'

'Everyone's entitled to some thinking-time,' he said evasively.

They were approaching another, thickly wooded coastline. A strong wind had blown up—the notorious summer *meltemi* which Sofie and Richard often talked about and which occasionally played havoc with inter-island shipping just when it was least expected. But this felt relatively gentle. It filled the sails, and blew them with a surge of speed towards the island.

A crescent of golden sand came into focus, protected by outcrops of rocks on either side, ringed with soft green pines and nestling in the shelter of a dramatically sloping hillside. The sails came down, with much hauling and winching, and Matt went below to switch on the motor.

She watched him absently, her mind racing. Thinking-time? Was he saying that he'd changed careers? But what about his talk of going off to do some business in Athens? Still the same old Matt, whatever he was trying to pretend. If there was a choice between staying in one place or moving on to another, he'd always be on the next plane out…

Steadily the yacht edged towards the island, stopping a hundred yards from the deserted shore. Matt dropped the anchor.

'I've been doing a spot of re-evaluating,' he added, in answer to her perplexed gaze. 'I'm going for a swim. Are you coming?'

Without waiting, he kicked off the white bermudas and strode to the steps at the rear of the boat. His charcoal-grey swimming-trunks were of the skimpy, clinging, silky variety, which left very little to the imagination. He looked over his shoulder, and caught her staring at the rock-hard plane of his stomach and the full, curved bulge of his crotch. To her horror she felt herself blushing fiercely.

'Don't look so embarrassed, Becky,' he taunted ruthlessly. 'I'm your husband, remember? You're entitled to stare, if that's what turns you on, my darling…'

Incensed, she jumped to her feet, her eyes blazing.

'You're so *arrogant*,' she burst out, giving him a push. Caught off balance, he teetered on the edge of the steps then fell with a resounding splash into the aquamarine water below. It only fuelled her anger to see him burst to the surface laughing, sweeping water from his face and hair. He swam strongly to the ladder and climbed back up with a determined gleam in his eyes.

'If it's rough games you want…' He grinned mercilessly, catching her as she started to dart away, lifting her easily into his arms. He was cool and wet from the sea, his over-long black hair plastered to his nape, his eyes bright with teasing hostility. 'Two can play…'

'Matt…please—' she was half frightened, half laughing '—I've still got my shorts and T-shirt on.'

'They'll dry,' he advised her mockingly, lifting her as high as he could, holding her well out over the rail of the yacht, and dropping her, backwards, into the water.

She'd always hated the feel of her head going right underwater. She hit the surface, plunged deeply beneath, then began to panic and thrash her way blindly back up. She broke into the sunlight, gasping and seething with indignation.

'You—you *brute*!' she spat, seeing Matt appear in the water at her side, his smile provocative. 'Pick on someone your own size!'

'You started it, Mrs Hawke.'

'Oh, you…!' Fiercely she splashed water at him, and had it returned in similar measure. The flash of white teeth in the dark face a few feet from her was so goadingly taunting that she felt her temper rocket.

'I *hate* you,' she managed, aiming a wild swipe at him and missing, ducking herself backwards into the sea instead. When she came up again, Matt was laughing. She swallowed some water, choked and began to swim as fast as she could back towards the boat. 'Just go away!' she hurled as she reached the safety of the ladder. 'Go to hell, Matt Hawke, and leave me alone!'

'OK. I'm going…' He sounded totally unrepentant, mocking, and infuriatingly amused.

She climbed out, and collapsed on deck. Matt was swimming powerfully away in the direction of the beach. She watched, seething, grappling for composure.

The dark head receded further and further, until she saw him climb out of the shallows and stroll lazily up the beach. He turned and looked across the water at her, where she sat on deck. Then he swivelled back and walked along the beach, away from her, finally disappearing from view behind a stand of pine trees.

The idea came to her like a bolt from the blue. Escape. Now was her chance to escape from this enforced trip with a man who drove her to distraction. She wasn't sure if she really intended to try to sail all the way back alone, she just knew that if she didn't take control, teach Matt Hawke a lesson for his domineering chauvinism, then she'd go insane with fury.

Without any clear idea of how she'd navigate her way back to Skopelos, she jumped down into the cockpit to find the ignition to start the engine. Then she hesitated. The anchor. First, the anchor…

As if possessed by some superhuman ability, she found herself instinctively copying what she'd watched Matt doing. Trembling with urgency, she hauled up the anchor and checked the beach. Checked the water. No sign of Matt. Throat dry with nerves, the pounding shudder of adrenalin shooting through her system, she started the engine, found the forward throttle…

The boat began to move, and she knew a split-second of sheer, blind terror as she began to steer her way back out of the enclosed cove.

The afternoon sun was dazzling as she stared ahead, trying to steady her nerves. What was she doing? she chided herself belatedly. Was she totally crazy? She should stop, turn back, abandon this hare-brained notion before it went any further.

A distant shout, resonant with fury, sounded behind her. Casting a fearful glance over her shoulder, she saw Matt running powerfully along the beach from the pine trees, saw him crash forcefully into the shallows and strike out in a dauntingly fast crawl. He was coming after her. The gut-wrenching sensation of being chased made her veer from panic to surrender. Panic won.

She found the throttle and increased speed, her palms damp with fright, her eyes momentarily blinded by the brilliance of the sun as she struggled to judge the exit from the cove. The wind had strengthened. The sea was surprisingly choppy the further she went out in the bay. It made steering the boat much harder than she'd imagined. She aimed

for the opening in the rocks, and gritted her teeth
optimistically.

One moment the sea looked clear, the next the
rock—a huge, jagged affair—had materialised out
of nowhere. The impact juddered with an ear-
splitting crunch, rending the air with horrifying
meaning. The engine strained, and stalled. The boat
lurched, and foundered. The wind gusted strongly,
and a wave lapped unkindly over the deck. The stern
dipped. It was taking on water, she realised helplessly. It had to be. Somewhere down below, in the
sump or the hold or whatever those parts of boats
were called.

What, in the name of heaven, did she do now?

'Oh, God, please… *Please*, God…no…!' Becky
gazed around her in mounting disbelief. What had
she done? Smashed Matt's boat? How could she
have been so stupid? Anger—revenge—was one
thing… But this? Matt would never forgive her for
this.

'Becky? Are you all right?'

'Yes.' She realised that Matt was about fifty yards
away, swimming with athletic strength towards her.
The wind had caught his voice and tossed it at her
in snatches.

'I'm OK, but I think the boat's sinking,' she
yelled back fearfully.

'Sweet *heaven*…' Matt's roar of fury sounded
across the water, amplified by the clearness of the

air, echoing off the silent, sweetly fragrant hillside, hitting her with the force of a physical attack. She tensed for the conflagration she expected, like a condemned prisoner waiting for execution…

'You crazy little bitch!' A few minutes later he came alongside, breathing ragged, the blaze in his eyes white-hot with fury. 'What the *hell* were you trying to do?'

'I was trying to sail your stupid boat.' She bit out the words, white-faced. 'I'm sorry, I didn't mean to hit a rock! The damn thing just—just jumped out at me!'

'Very amusing. Like lamp-posts have a habit of doing in front of incompetent motorists, I suppose?' He'd hauled himself up by the brass railing, which was now at a very unhealthy angle indeed as the boat pitched miserably to the right.

She clung to the side as he ducked grimly below, wincing as his rapid movements in the saloon caused the boat to grind harshly on the rock. She'd never felt such a mixture of guilt, anger and resentment.

When Matt reappeared he was carrying two bulging rucksacks, which he dumped on the deck. His face was grimly sardonic.

'Can you mend it?' she begged quickly, squeezing her hands tightly behind her back. She felt like a naughty child caught smashing the best china, she realised with a twinge of bitter humour.

'It's too far gone,' he said coolly. 'The radio's out. The engine's knackered. The best we can do is salvage the dinghy from the back and row to the beach with as much gear as possible.'

'Couldn't we just use the dinghy to sail round the coast—find some civilisation?'

'First, this end of the island is uninhabited apart from the odd goatherd living in a one-roomed hut. Second, with this wind blowing up we'd be much safer on dry land than floating around on the sea in a small dinghy.' He handed her an empty cool-bag with a jerk of impatience. 'Fill that with as much food as you can from the fridge, and hurry up.'

She flinched at the harsh order, but took the bag in silence and did as he said. Now wasn't the time for complaining about his rudeness. Matt, she told herself uneasily, had every right to be a trifle touchy right at this minute.

When she emerged, he was standing in the dinghy, loading the rucksacks and a large holdall, which looked as if it might contain sleeping-bags.

He took the cool-bag of food from her, and then held up his hand to help her down.

'We'll just hope that the weight of all this doesn't sink the dinghy before we get to the beach,' he commented ominously smoothly.

Swallowing hard, she huddled in the small boat, watching Matt hauling with suppressed fury on the oars.

The trip across the bay, at least, ended success-
fully. Dragging the dinghy up the wet sand, they off-
loaded the supplies and dumped them in a forlorn
pile in the middle of the beach.

Becky looked at Matt.

'I'm really sorry,' she said quietly.

'I'll bet you are. Sorry at the prospect of spending
an uncomfortable night on the beach.'

'Matt, it was an accident...'

'So I gather.' His gaze was blazingly sarcastic. 'I
knew you were misguided, Becky, but I didn't think
you were certifiable!'

'It's your own damn fault,' she flared indignantly,
sitting down in the warm sand with a thud. 'If you
hadn't *kidnapped* me none of this would have happened.'

He gazed down at her for a few moments, his
expression darkly unreadable. Then he gave a short
laugh.

'OK. Does this make us quits?' he asked tersely.
'I kidnap you; you sink my boat?'

She lifted her shoulders in a slight shrug. She was
tense and miserable, in spite of the warmth of the
sun and the peaceful beauty of her surroundings.
The only thing to mar the perfection of the setting
was the wind, flicking sand into her face as it gusted
along the beach. She wriggled out of the uncomfortably wet T-shirt and shorts, and laid them carefully on the sand to dry in the sun.

'It hasn't *quite* sunk...' she began tentatively. As she spoke there was a groaning, sucking sound from out in the bay. They both looked on in silence as thirty feet and thousands of pounds' worth of luxury yacht tilted drunkenly into the air, poised there a few seconds as if to wave goodbye, then lurched into a capsized position, half in, half out of the water.

'You were saying?' he prompted caustically.

She found that she was winding her hair nervously round her finger. Horror engulfed her. She hardly dared look at Matt's face. The hostile fury and disbelief were only too easy to imagine.

She tried a cautious touch of humour. 'You can always bank the insurance money. And three months at sea is long enough for anyone, isn't it?'

'Rebecca...' She froze at the note in his voice.

'Mmm?'

'I'm suppresssing the strong desire to lynch you from the nearest pine tree. Don't push your luck.'

'Murder isn't the answer,' she fenced warily, standing up and dusting the wet sand off the back of her swimsuit. 'Unless you think avenging the loss of your beloved boat is worth a life sentence?'

With a furious lunge, he grabbed her and hauled her to him. 'You must be the most idiotic, empty-headed little *bimbo* I've ever had the misfortune to meet.'

'*Bimbo*...?' she began hotly, then choked on the outraged protest as he dropped his head and kissed her. He kissed her with punishing demand, muffling her words back in her throat. She struggled, and he tightened his hold. It was like being caught in a steel trap, pinned against him, every hard line of his body searing her with heat.

'You brute…bully… Let go of me…' she managed to spit, before he covered her mouth again. Lifting her in his arms, he strode towards the sea. In a flurry of flailing arms she found herself deposited abruptly in the warm shallows, her swimsuit unzipped and peeled away from her breasts. Her nipples sprang up in traitorous response as he let his lidded gaze roam over her nakedness.

Furious with herself, as well as with Matt, she hit out at him. She connected with the side of his jaw, then found herself flattened, pinned to the wet sand as Matt cupped her swelling softness in his hands, carressing the sensitive peaks with restrained ferocity.

'Matt…stop it, please…' From somewhere among the aggression and the wildcat defence came the flames of need. Desire was shooting through her nervous system like a fireball.

'Matt, *please*!' she repeated weakly, but she already suspected that her defiance lacked conviction.

'Let's forget the games, shall we?' His voice was raw, huskily aggressive, thick with desire, anger, and a host of dangerous emotions that she couldn't begin to decipher. 'I still want you. And you still

want me.' He gave her an abrupt, taut shake, his
banked-down fury visible in the rigid set of his face.
'I can feel you do, Becky...'

Her face hot, she gazed up at him helplessly. She
was enraged, humiliated, but burning up with need.
She was shaking all over. Matt was like a coiled
spring. Like a time bomb ticking over her. The time
they'd spent apart seemed to contract and disappear.
The feeling was as raw, as undeniable now as it had
been that first unforgettable night in her bedsit.

'Is this payment for the boat?' she whispered
tautly. She was quivering all over. He didn't bother
to reply. But he assertively trapped her beneath him
with one powerful thigh, and bent to take one rosy
nipple in his mouth. Convulsively she arched her
back as he tugged hungrily, licked and stroked with
his tongue, and moved to the other breast to arouse
and inflame in the same skilful fashion.

There had always been something about the way
he made love to her, she shuddered despairingly.
Something irresistible. Something which made her
feel intensely feminine, softly vulnerable, overwhelmingly desirable.

He'd been her first lover. Whatever the rights and
wrongs of the past, no other man had ever come
close to this nameless havoc that Matt could wreak
with a single touch. No other man had a way of
making her feel like a cordon bleu meal being of-
fered to a starving gourmet...

But now there was a vengeful air of barbarism, a sense of tightly controlled violence that made her shiver, all the way down to her toes, with a mixture of fear and hunger.

'This,' he murmured thickly, easing the swimsuit down to strip it decisively from her trembling hips, exposing the curve of her buttocks, the flatness of her stomach, the secret amber triangle, baring her whole body to his lidded appraisal, 'is payment for two years of hell.'

She wrenched in her breath. He was calling in debts, then taking what he misguidedly saw as his due. Anger mounted, but he was already raking bold, predatory fingers down her body, smoothing with possessive demand all the way down to her inner thighs. Panic was giving way to the sinking, treacherous blindness of desire.

As if he read her mind, or the crazy workings of her heart, his tightly leashed assault became sharper, more concentrated.

'Admit it,' he goaded, shuddering with his own need. 'Admit that you want this as much as I do, Becky.'

Matt's eyes were mesmerising. Dark with sexual hunger, the pupils dilated, almost filling the brilliance of the blue with the shadow of sensuality.

'I don't know... Maybe I do...but not like this, Matt...'

She couldn't help it. Tears, hot and incriminating,

stung her eyes. The emotion overwhelming her was partly humiliation, partly agonising, debilitating pain, devastating her with its unexpectedness. Matt hated her. She could feel it in the way he touched her—the way he was projecting his own anger on to her.

He stopped moving for a few seconds, his lidded gaze intent on her flushed face. The glitter of raw emotion which she saw there almost annihilated her. For a second she looked into his eyes and saw torment—saw right inside, into his soul, and felt that she understood him, on some subconscious level, for the first time since she'd known him.

She was lost, abruptly reaching up for him, letting her fingers caress the hard strength of his shoulders, indulging in the wanton pleasure of the damp, thick hair at his nape.

'Show me,' he grated hoarsely, dropping a string of sensual, arousing, blatantly sexual kisses on her parted lips. 'Show me how much you want this...'

She was beyond reason, beyond caution. Shivering with feverish impatience, she let her hands rediscover every glorious line of him, revelling in the hollows and bulges of muscled steel, trembling as each caress drew a shudder of male hunger in response.

'Make love to me, Matt.' The words were wrenched from her. Bitterly, but clearly. She couldn't believe that she was hearing herself. She couldn't believe that this was really happening…

'Becky… Oh, God, Becky…' The force of his passion engulfed her. He lost control. With a choked cry of surrender, she was spread-eagled in the lapping water, her thighs roughly parted, her smallest secrets mercilessly exposed. She cried out as he raked her body with a fierce tenderness, invading those secrets at the deepest level, his fingers expertly circling the tight nub of passion in the softness of her sex, coaxing her to such melting wantonness that she gave an involuntary shriek of reaction.

'Shh…you'll frighten the fishes,' he taunted raggedly, moving to take full possession of her.

His forceful thrust was so invasive, so overwhelming, that she felt a wave of dizziness overtake her. And then everything homed in, focused, concentrated on that unique, thrusting, age-old rhythm—man and woman, male and female, pleasure and anger, bittersweet intimacy. The ripples of reaction widened and intensified until she felt as if she was on the wild edge of a storm, the force mounting to such a pitch that it threatened to wipe her out completely in its chaotic destruction.

The sea had roughened, but the late afternoon sun was still warm. Naked, abandoned as a mermaid, she lay half in, half out of the water, Matt's hard body sprawled at her side, her eyes closed.

She tried very hard to suppress the ripples of euphoria still twanging through her. It didn't seem to matter for the moment that she'd broken her vow to herself, that she'd let him steamroller her into submission. It had been a mutual defeat, or a mutual victory. Her cool, disinterested husband still found her desirable—small comfort, totally irrelevent in the grand scheme of things, but somehow it mattered.

Tentatively she twisted her head to look at him. She'd imagined that he was dozing, but his eyes were open, narrowed tautly on the horizon. The hostility in his gaze as he switched the narrow blue stare towards her made her heart tighten.

Colour rushed to her face, then drained. Clearing her throat, she managed a casual shrug.

'I gather the payment wasn't enough, then?' she taunted, bleakly sarcastic.

His eyes were shuttered as he glanced up and down her body.

'No,' he agreed quietly. With a flex of muscle, he got to his feet and calmly pulled on his swimming trunks. He eyed her with a smoky glint of anger. 'You're right. It wasn't nearly enough.'

CHAPTER SIX

'So...WHAT do we do now?' Becky risked a tentative glance at Matt. They'd finished a picnic meal of bread, cheese and peaches, and the atmosphere was so arctic that she found it hard to believe that they were sitting on a sun-warmed beach, shaded by softly wind-blown pine trees, with the crickets shrilling their hypnotic song from the rugged hillside surrounding them.

He glanced at his watch, his expression implacable.

'Let's examine the options,' he said, his voice devoid of emotion. 'It's too late for us both to start walking. There's no guarantee we'd find your "civilisation" before dark. Your state of health is dubious, so that needs to be taken into account in any distance we cover—'

'I'm not an invalid,' she protested, annoyed. Matt ignored her.

'It's too windy to take the dinghy out to sea. We camp here for the night. But I'll hike inland a few miles before then—see if I come across anything.'

She stared at him in mounting dismay. He'd

hinted at this earlier, but for some reason she'd assumed that one of them would conveniently come up with some alternative.

'I suppose camping here for the night can't be worse than sleeping in a mosquito-ridden rescue centre in Ethiopa,' she agreed calmly. 'But if you're walking anywhere I'm coming too!'

'You're staying here,' he informed her abruptly. 'I'll be quicker on my own.'

Thrusting her hands into the pockets of the dried-out green shorts, she lifted her chin and fixed him with a steady gaze.

'I can walk fast enough. I'm feeling quite a lot better—'

'One of us needs to stay here with the gear. And to attract attention if any boats pass.'

'But if you found somewhere we could stay, you'd have to come all the way back for me!'

'Just for once, will you do as you're told?'

The harshness in his voice made her stiffen indignantly. But she knew when to admit defeat.

'Whatever you say, Boss Man,' she murmured coolly. 'Where are we, anyway?'

'Skyros.'

'*Skyros*? Are you sure?'

A gleam of reluctant amusement tinged the hard blue gaze.

'Yes, Becky, I'm sure. Until a couple of hours

ago I was the proud possessor of a map and compass that told me so.'

She blushed again. She couldn't stop herself. Sinking Matt's boat was like a nightmare—something she'd undoubtedly done but couldn't quite bring herself to believe.

'But surely Skyros has holiday resorts, an airport...'

'It does. That doesn't mean we've ended up within hailing distance of any of them. Skyros is quite a big island. It's very sparsely populated, but if you see any passing planes or holidaymakers be sure to give them a shout.'

She clenched her fists to suppress the urge to hit him.

'Don't worry, I will.'

He shot her a thoughtful look, but didn't bother to comment. He collected the plates they'd used and took them down to rinse them swiftly in the sea. Then he put a bottle of water in one of the empty rucksacks, and narrowed a cool glance at her as she sat in the shade of the pine tree.

'I'll be back soon,' he said non-committally, before setting off at an athletic-looking lope. She watched him go, lithe and muscular in the black T-shirt he'd pulled on over his white bermudas, until he was out of sight behind the trees up the steep hillside.

Alone, she leaned with her back to the tree. The

meltemi had picked up even more, hissing through the pines, flicking crests on the waves in the bay. Now that Matt had gone, the beach seemed deathly quiet, unbearably lonely. She must be mad, she told herself crossly, to prefer being in Matt's coldly aloof company to relaxing here in the peace and solitude.

A huge, luminous green cricket whirred past and stopped on the next tree. She watched it absently, thinking of the flies and the insects in Africa. After Africa, there was nothing too fearsome about the average European insect, she realised wryly. She'd done a lot of maturing in her time out there. A lot of growing up—emotional growing-up…or so she'd thought.

But now, being with Matt again, it had abruptly struck her that she'd resolved nothing, achieved nothing in her time apart from him. She was still a mass of seething insecurities.

Something Sofie had said came back to her with a jolt as she flicked sand off her thighs. 'You and Matt should have a lot in common—you both think the world's against you.'

Becky stared at the mauve-blue horizon. The sun was starting to sink. The light was tinged with gold; the shadows were lengthening.

It occurred to her that she'd never fully under-stood that remark of Sofie's. Matt had always breezed through life as if he needed no convincing that the world was well and truly at his well-heeled feet. The only background they shared, she thought drily, was an overdose of tragedy and trauma, and the absence of mothers and fathers in the correct quantities and of the desired quality.

Matt had never talked much about his family, or much about his past, but he and Richard had read modern languages together at Oxford and become friends, so Sofie had been able to provide the information. His mother had walked out on the family when Matt was twelve, and his father had promptly succumbed to a breakdown, remaining a shadow of his former self until he'd died.

As for her, when their parents had died in a road accident when she was sixteen Sofie had been wonderful—caring and supportive. She and Richard had helped her to get to university, and supported her until the extra income from part-time modelling made her financially independent. But she sometimes felt as if she was lurching involuntarily from one emotional crisis to another. Was everyone's life like this? Or did she attract emotional turmoil like a magnet?

Not all the crises had been bad, she reflected cautiously. There'd been highs and lows. The highest of all highs had been meeting Matt, then discovering she was carrying his baby—Matt's baby... The lowest had been realising what she should have realised all along—that the baby had been the only reason he'd married her. And once that reason had been taken away the void left behind had been so great that no amount of pretence, or play-acting, or determination to make things work would ever have filled the gaping hole…

In the awful weeks following her miscarriage, she'd sunk into depression. Losing the baby had battered her hormones, but it was grasping the truth about her marriage that had delivered the knock-out blow. She'd felt as if she and Matt had survived an earthquake but ended up on separate scraps of land, floating opposite ways, with no way of controlling their directions to get back to where they'd started.

Had she driven him away by her insecurity, her introspection? No. He'd been separating himself mentally, emotionally, in any case. He'd been painfully eager to leave her alone in Hampstead and jump on the next international flight. He'd married her to give his child a legitimate start in life. And then there'd been no need, after all. How he must have seethed with frustration, trapped with her while the beautiful Su-Lin waited for him in Hong Kong…

Ted had been a good friend. The modelling agency had tried several times to tempt her back to work for them, but she'd lost any desire to model, just as she'd lost the motivation to pick up her degree course again. All she'd wanted was Matt's love, and it had been a lie. It had never existed in the form she'd so romantically imagined.

And then she'd had the letter from Su-Lin's family. The confirmation of her secret fears, it had been formal, politely phrased, and somehow all the more deadly poisonous for being so. Matt and Su-Lin had intended to marry before Becky inconvenienced them all by conceiving. The best thing she could do for all concerned, now that the pregnancy was at an end, was to bow out gracefully.

She closed her eyes, anger and misery flooding her all over again. If only Matt had stayed away from her. She'd kept her distance for two years, unable to face the sordid fight for divorce by naming Su-Lin as the other woman. Now, just when a divorce was possible by mutual consent, he had to come marching arrogantly back into her life. Why? What did he hope to gain? Apart from the acute male satisfaction of sexual possession to salve his injured pride? And he'd won that fight, she reflected bitterly. He'd won.

The shameful ecstasy of their passionate coming-together melted back through her as she thought about it. She pushed the memory ruthlessly away.

He'd won, but only because she'd been feeling so wretchedly guilty about his boat, she told herself firmly. It had been a meaningless, mechanical, stress-release activity—nothing more.

Tiredness washed over her, and she settled against the tree, leaning her head back. It hadn't meant anything, she reassured herself sleepily. It made no difference how easily he could arouse her to mindless pleasure; she didn't care about him any longer. She felt nothing for him. Nothing at all. And nothing was going to change that...

She opened her eyes again, feeling disorientated. She'd fallen asleep, and it was nearly dark. Stiff with sitting so long, she climbed awkwardly to her feet, brushed herself down, and glanced up and down the beach. No sign of Matt. Where on earth was he?

She emerged from the trees and stood alone, feeling a mounting sense of anxiety. Their gear was still piled at the top of the beach. The wind had dropped, as it so often seemed to at nightfall. A sickle-shaped moon hung in a Prussian blue sky and the sea was now so calm that she could see an almost perfect mirror image of it in the black surface of the water.

Turning to stare back up the hillside, she felt a prickle of unease. The trees crowding up the slopes had lost their soft, daytime greenness and now looked darkly sinister. The crickets' song sounded more menacing than hypnotic.

What could have happened to Matt? Alarm began to replace anxiety. Had he had an accident? Common sense told her that it was unlikely, but she couldn't stop her visions of him lying at the foot of a ravine, unconscious...or worse...

Which way should she go and look? She chewed distractedly on her lip, her mind racing, her heart starting to thud. This was crazy. It could end up in *Midsummer Night's Dream*-style, with one person disappearing into the dark woods and the other appearing, round and round in circles…

The silence pressed in. Taking a deep breath, she opened her mouth to yell Matt's name, and then nearly died of shock as a strong hand covered her mouth, and she was grabbed tightly from behind.

'Don't worry, it's only me.' He grinned, spinning her round.

Heat flared through her. Her temper exploded. She started to tremble uncontrollably.

'Of all the childish tricks!' she began passionately. 'I was worried sick about you! And… And you—you creep up behind me and…'

'Poor little Becky,' he taunted mockingly. 'But I'm touched that you were worried about me. I didn't think you cared if I lived or died.'

She glared at him.

'Normally, I don't,' she corrected herself crossly, stepping back and folding her arms defensively across her chest. 'But until we get out of this mess I'd rather you lived, thanks all the same.'

'Until I've been of requisite use to you?' Matt's deep voice was silkily calm.

'Precisely.'

'You haven't by any chance forgotten that you got us *into* this mess?'

She caught her breath. 'Indirectly, I admit—'

'*Indirectly*?' His narrowed gaze glittered with disbelief. 'How do you figure that one, Mrs Hawke?'

'You forced me into this stupid sailing trip! Remember?'

'You walked out on our marriage. Remember?'

There was a silence. The crickets were the only sound as they stared at each other.

'So...forget the hypocritical claim of looking after me, of making me have a rest and get fit! This *was* revenge, wasn't it? You forced me to go sailing with you to demonstrate how powerful you are!'

'I'm not feeling too powerful right now,' he mocked flatly. 'Not with my boat floating upside-down in the bay.'

'So I'm the major villain now?' she countered bitterly, her voice a fraction unsteady. 'Fine. What do I have to do as penance this time?'

'It won't go very far towards bringing my yacht back, but you could start by collecting some wood.' There was a blandness in his tone suddenly.

'Wood?' She gazed at him blankly.

'For a fire.' Matt's voice held the elaborate patience of the wise addressing the foolish.

'*Right.*' She spun round and walked stiffly up to the trees, beginning to pick up pine-cones and twigs, gathering them in a pile in her arms and carrying them back to the designated camp. When the mound was big enough she marched over to Matt, and dusted her hands down triumphantly.

'There. One fire. Anything else? Would you like me to dive for fish with a knife between my teeth?'

'Now that might be entertaining.' He'd fetched a box of matches from one of the rucksacks and was squatting down to arrange the twigs in a small wigwam shape to start the fire. She bit back her furious retort, and watched in reluctant curiosity.

'Don't tell me,' she said at last, 'that I was married to you for six months and you never even told me you used to be a Boy Scout?'

'That's right.' His glance up at her held a fraction less coolness. 'Weren't you a Girl Guide?'

She shook her head with a short laugh.

'Brownies was as far as I got.'

'Insufficient training for surviving on deserted Greek island beaches.' He shook his head in disapproval.

'True. But we did learn to make toast without burning our fingers on the toaster.'

'Invaluable.' He straightened up, his face deadpan as he met her eyes. 'Damn, I forgot to pack the toaster.'

She laughed, and with a brief grimace he laughed too. A slight warmth crept into the air between them for the first time.

'Matt...' Suddenly her voice sounded husky. She cleared her throat. 'I really am terribly sorry about your boat. Will you believe me?'

His gaze was speculative as he watched her.

'OK. I believe you.'

Expelling her breath heavily, she sat down, cross-legged, in front of the crackle of flame. After a second's pause Matt sat down too, knees bent up and spread wide, elbows on his knees. His face looked darkly attractive in the flickering firelight.

'Are you hungry?' he asked.

'Not really. Are you?'

'Nope.'

She stared at the fire for a while, trying to gather her thoughts together.

'Did you mean it about sailing around for the last three months?' she asked quietly.

'Yes, I meant it. That's exactly what I've been doing. Mostly alone. Sometimes with company.'

'What about your job?'

He shrugged slightly. 'Even die-hard workaholics like me take time off. Given the necessary impetus.'

She felt her throat dry slightly.

'The necessary impetus being...?'

Matt was silent for so long that she decided he obviously wasn't going to answer. Finally, he said, 'To re-evaluate. Like I said.'

'But something must have happened,' she persisted warily. She felt as if she was tiptoeing over egg-shells. Dragging anything personal out of Matt Hawke had always been like this. 'Something to trigger it off...?'

'Yes, it did. I took a long look in the mirror one day, in the Club Class lounge of British Airways. I didn't like what I saw.'

'What did you think was wrong with what you saw?'

'The guy had no soul.' He grinned bleakly. 'He looked like the kind of shallow bastard who might neglect his wife.'

Becky felt her breathing constrict in her chest. Emotion was wrenching through her, with twists of physical pain.

'So you took to the sea?'

'Yup. I did a circuit of the Dodecanese, the Cyclades and the Saronic Gulf Islands, before I had to admit that the Northern Sporades held the main attraction.'

'Cooler weather?'

'Some link with my missing wife,' he supplied softly. 'If we ignore Richard and Sofie's wedding as our first introduction, we met on Skopelos—or had you forgotten?'

She caught her breath in a sharp, agonised intake.

'Of course I hadn't forgotten!' she whispered. 'Just because our—our marriage didn't work out doesn't mean I developed amnesia!'

'Quite. Nor me.' She couldn't tell what he was thinking. His voice was even, lacking expression. 'It's surprising how much remembering gets done, sailing around on your own.'

'Yes.'

'How was it in Africa?' There was an ironic trace

in his voice. She watched him reaching to push a stick further into the fire.

'Similar...in terms of thinking,' she agreed, rather stiffly.

'Our marriage wasn't all bad, was it, Becky?'

She looked at him in sudden confusion. His tone was still expressionless. His eyes were unreadable. She shook her head slowly.

'No...the first few weeks were—were good!' There was deliberate irony in her voice, but it was true. The beginning of their marriage had been perfect, she recalled painfully. She'd naïvely thought that she'd found her soul mate. And everything had been so exciting. Matt had been so unpredictable.

Their honeymoon had started in the chilly wildness of the Outer Hebrides, where they had discovered a shared taste for windswept hillsides and crackling log fires. Then without warning he'd whisked her off to the Seychelles, where they'd relaxed in the luxurious contrasting heat, swimming and playing backgammon and Scrabble but spending most of the time making love in their beautiful hotel room.

She glanced at him with a wary smile. 'I used to think we had a lot in common, as a matter of fact. Tastes in holidays, theatre, films, humour...'

'Opera?' He reminded her with a bleak grin. 'Remember *L'Elisir d'amore*? I fell asleep...'

She found herself laughing suddenly.

'And fell off your chair in the box. How could I forget?'

'I was jet-lagged.'

'You were *always* jet-lagged.'

There was a brief pause. The laughter had gone.

'You know, this is so strange,' she said quietly, 'I feel as if we're the only people left in the world, sitting here round this little camp-fire.'

'Cue for a song, isn't it?' There was a stronger bitterness in his voice now, in spite of the slight thaw between them. 'Would you marry me again, Becky? If I was the only male left in the world?'

She felt herself go very still. Her heart began thumping uncomfortably.

'What do you think?' she managed at last.

'I think you'd probably need your beautiful little head read.' He abruptly uncoiled, straightening up and walking down towards the sea.

Uncertainly, she watched him go. She was frozen there, trapped by pride and doubt. And fear. There was something disturbing, something raw and subtly dangerous about this conversation. She had the shaky feeling that she might say something she'd eternally regret.

But she couldn't stop herself. She followed him down to the shoreline. A ferry was ploughing past in the distance, lights twinkling. The only sound was the lap and hiss of the waves on the dark sand and pebbles.

'Matt…what did you mean?'

'I meant that I wasn't ready to marry anyone when we married.'

'But you did marry me.' She kept her voice level with supreme self-control. Why was she putting herself through this emotional mangle? Maybe she'd had too much sun…

'So I did. And I screwed up, didn't I?' The glance he turned her way was bleakly self-mocking. For some reason it tugged at her heart.

'Why? Why did you marry me, Matt?'

He turned to face her. His expression was hard and mocking in the moonlight.

'You know why, Becky,' he mocked bleakly. 'You've told me often enough. I married you because you were pregnant.'

'Matt…' The pain inside, the rush of anguish, was too strong to suppress. Unthinkingly, she reached her hand out to touch his face. With a muttered curse, he pulled her with rough urgency into his arms. A shudder went through him as he held her there, tightly cradled. Closing her eyes, she put her arms round him, breathing in the scent of him, her body reacting to his without her volition. He closed what little gap remained between them, ducked his head and found her mouth with his.

'Becky…' He broke off the kiss, his hands cupping her face. 'Hell, I don't know how we made such a mess of things.'

'Nor do I.'

His kiss, when he dropped his head again, was gentle, searching her lips. His tenderness was in such contrast to their previous lovemaking that she felt her senses swim.

'Matt… Oh, Matt…' Her husky whisper brought his arms down around her in a possessive scoop. She was lifted and carried with suppressed urgency back up the shadowy beach to the fire. The sleeping-bags had been spread out there, and he drew her down on the quilted surface, his hands smoothing and seeking over the whole quivering length of her body with a contained kind of desperation.

Suddenly Becky's whole perception tilted and spun into another dimension. Nothing else mattered. Their past, their future, the impossible problems of their relationship—everything faded. Her only pre-occupation was this warmth, this anguished flood of gentle sensuality. The only compelling need was the touch of Matt's hands, and the stubborn pulse of response in her bloodstream.

'I still want you, Becky.' He grated the words harshly, as if the admission hurt.

'I know,' she whispered on a ragged laugh. 'Make love to me again, Matt…but not to punish me this time…'

'*Oh, God*, Becky.'

His groan sent her pulse-rate rocketing. She let her fingers stroke his face, rake hungrily through the thickness of his hair, grasp the taut slope of his shoulders. With a moan of desire she moulded herself against him, running her hands down to push up the black T-shirt. The lean planes and angles of his body, the silken warmth of his skin and the coarseness of his body hair made her senses tingle.

'This feels so good,' he breathed, caressing the slender length of her thighs. Impatiently he was stripping off his bermudas, swimming-trunks and T-shirt, beginning to strip her clothes from her until she was naked and trembling beneath him. But then he pulled her forcefully over to straddle him, and the sensations of his lean body beneath her parted thighs made her gasp with shocked pleasure.

Matt gave a low, triumphant laugh as he grasped the soft curve of her hips. 'We might have incompatible characters, sweetheart, but physically nothing beats this.'

'Not even Su-Lin?' The shaky whisper was involuntary. She had no idea why she had felt compelled to say it. Matt froze like a statue beneath her. Abruptly the warmth had gone. The tenderness became suppressed anger.

'I wouldn't know,' he murmured ruthlessly. Lifting her a fraction, he plunged her down on to his rigid maleness, so that she gave a choked scream of response. 'I never did this with Su-Lin...'

The warm night, the velvety darkness and the thin, sickle-shaped moon seemed to swim in and out of her awareness as the beat of desire, the wild roar of her senses took over, completely engulfing her. Afterwards, what seemed like an endless space of time later, she stirred cautiously in the hard constraint of his arms.

'Do you have to do that?' she managed quietly.

'Do what?'

'Make love to me as if you hate me.' There was a quiver of emotion in her voice, and she bit her lip. She wouldn't cry. She wouldn't give him the satisfaction of reducing her to tears.

Matt was silent. She turned to look at him. In the darkness his features looked sombre, shadowed, disturbingly compelling.

'Did I hurt you?'

A wave of heat flooded her face as he studied her with that intent, dispassionate gaze.

'Not physically… But…'

'I don't hate you, Becky.' His voice was a soft drawl, masking his feelings.

'It feels as if you do.'

'Then you're mistaken.' There was a cool finality in his voice which chilled her.

She moved away from him, wriggled into her sleeping-bag and pulled it closely around her ears. She felt utterly humiliated and dejected, and more forlorn and alone than at any time over the last two years of their separation.

CHAPTER SEVEN

THE Flying Dolphin inter-island hydrofoil swooped around the headland towards Skopelos harbour, and reduced speed with a drone like an aircraft coming in to land.

'There we are, Mrs Hawke—civilisation.'

Matt's cool murmur made her stiffen slightly. Their conversation, since the fiasco of their love-making the night before, had been stilted to say the least. And the atmosphere between them hadn't been improved by her discovery that Matt, and the fishermen who'd rescued them, had met the night before, on his reconnoitre mission. Their uncomfortable night on the beach had been unnecessary.

'I suppose you just wanted me to pay for sinking the boat?' she'd accused him furiously, gathering their gear together as the small fishing boat waited to take them round to the island's main port to catch the hydrofoil. She'd slept badly, haunted by dreams, and woken stiff and bad-tempered, feeling as wrecked as the yacht. He'd shrugged, with that infuriatingly bland expression which told her nothing.

'I thought you enjoyed it,' he teased softly.

'Camp-fires, making love in the moonlight—very romantic.'

'That wasn't making love. It was venting your anger, flexing your power complex!'

'Are you telling me you felt nothing?' he'd goaded, watching her speculatively, 'Because you can't fool me, Becky. You were just as involved as I was.'

She gave him a wary glance now as they stepped from the air-conditioned coolness of the Flying Dolphin on to the sun-baked quayside in Skopelos. Even when he was at his most suave and business-like, dressed for the boardroom, Matt habitually had a rather piratical air about him, with his thick black hair and his hard blue eyes and his five o'clock shadow, which he ruthlessly tamed to an acceptable bluish-black shading around his jaw.

Today, though, after their escapades on Skyros, he looked positively villainous. The five o'clock shadow was anything but tame. It was a rough, mas-culine stubble, of the type which would probably be worshipped by fans of macho rock-guitarists. Mixed with his height, his lean muscularity, and the unholy glint of grim amusement in his expression, his ap-pearance was making her feel rather breathless and nervous.

'Maybe it's unrealistic of me to ask you to behave like a gentleman,' she began firmly, 'when you look like a thug...'

'*Efharisto, kyria,*' he murmured wryly, sketching a mock bow.

'But now that we're back, maybe we can agree to forget all about what happened on—on the boat trip, and…'

'And set divorce proceedings in motion?' he supplied coolly.

'Yes. Exactly.'

There was a brief, reflective pause. Matt's gaze was unreadable.

'You were right,' he agreed flatly. Turning to stroll in the direction of Sofie's and Richard's house, he glanced back at her with a cool smile. She followed him in mounting alarm.

'What do you mean I was right?' she demanded crossly.

'Definitely unrealistic.'

'Matt!'

'We'll talk about this later, when we've made good use of hot showers and an enormous breakfast.'

'It's lunchtime. Besides, what is there to talk about?'

'Desertion. Wilful damage of property…' They'd reached the house, and Sofie, primed by a telephone call from Skyros, was opening the door. Becky was opening her mouth to argue fiercely, but shut it again as she met her sister's cautious smile.

'Hello—did you enjoy your unexpected trip?'

'She had a wonderful time,' Matt supplied briefly, seeing Becky's speechless reaction. 'Do you mind if we take over your bathrooms and telephone for a while, Sofie?'

With a slight laugh, she shook her head and ushered them inside. Becky found herself showering off the sand and salt in the en-suite bathroom in Sofie's room, while Matt used the one adjoining her own room.

To describe her mood as seething would be a severe understatement, she reflected tautly. Why couldn't the hateful man understand that he wasn't *wanted*? That she'd made the decision to get him out of her life, and she hadn't made it rashly or lightly? That his arrogant invasion of her privacy was unforgivable?

And why did Sofie have to treat him like one of the family?

It was one thing for Richard to greet Matt with great enthusiasm—round face alight, his brown eyes gleaming with pleasure, the way he'd been when they'd bumped into him just now in the hall—he and Matt were old friends. But Sofie was her sister. Why couldn't she take *sides* a little, for heaven's sake?

Her nervous system felt as if it had taken quite a beating over the past forty-eight hours. But when she was faced with Matt's company again, over a late lunch at a taverna on the quay, she realised with a lurch of dismay that her battle was far from over.

'I have to attend to some important business in Athens. I want you to come with me,' he stated calmly, pouring some more mineral water into her glass, and taking another mouthful of his red wine.

The sun was dappling through the plane trees above them, making his face even harder to read than normal.

'*Me*? Come with you to Athens! No way!' She pushed away what was left of her meal—the excellent Skopelos cheese pie of crunchy filo pastry and feta that she'd chosen and hardly tasted.

'That's not the answer I wanted to hear, Becky.'

She lifted her head abruptly, and met a very hard gleam of blue beneath lazily narrowed eyelids. Her throat dried. What now? What, apart from the sordid obvious, could Matt possibly want with her in Athens?

At the waterside, rows of fishing boats, private yachts and luxury launches bobbed side by side. Beyond stretched the turquoise circle of the bay, ringed with olive-clad hills, and gilded with translucent sunlight. The uneven, whitewashed walls of an ancient monastery glistened at the end of the seafront.

She thought of Matt's boat, lolling sadly on its face in the deserted cove on Skyros, and winced in memory. Some of his many telephone calls this morning had been in connection with the boat, she knew. Salvaging it, repairing it, or just simply checking on the insurance? As Matt was fluent in Greek and she spoke none, she wasn't too sure of the outcome. On the whole, she had to admit, he seemed to have taken the loss of his boat remarkably well.

Glancing back at him, clean-shaven, black hair falling thick and shiny to the base of his neck, relaxed and lethally attractive in jeans and white T-shirt, her heart tightened in her chest.

Pride and a need to boost her self-confidence had inspired her to make an effort with her own appearance since they'd got back. Her body tingled pleasantly with floral-scented shower-gel and cologne; her honey-brown hair hung, freshly-washed and bouncy, past her shoulders; her sage-green cotton jersey dress clung in all the right places, emphasising her extreme slenderness. She'd caught the sun on the boat and her skin had taken on a healthier golden glow. Nervously she crossed one slim, tanned leg over the other, and tried to keep her concentration centred on deflecting Matt's overpowering personality.

'Perhaps, in view of the complete breakdown of our marriage to date, and my desire for a divorce, you'd like to explain why you could possibly have imagined that I'd say yes?' she enquired, picking her words with elaborate care, her tone sweetly reasonable.

Matt regarded her levelly. The waiter came to clear their plates, scooping away the remains of Matt's grilled sole and fries along with her leftovers. She declined the suggestion of pudding.

'Just coffee, please,' Matt murmured, switching that disconcerting gaze back to her. 'I'm being invited to dinner with the people I'm going to be working for on a consultancy basis. You're my wife; I'd appreciate your company.'

She felt as if she'd been stung. Stiff with indignation, she gripped the wicker arms of her chair.

'Matt, I hardly believe I'm hearing this. This is ridiculous.'

'You owe me.'

She felt her breath leave her lungs in a sharp hiss. The silence which followed this cool statement seemed to resound with tension.

'I see,' she managed tightly. She moistened her lips, stiffening as she felt Matt's eyes on the small movement. 'At least, I think I'm beginning to see. Are you actually trying to—to *shame* me into coming to Athens with you? Because of your blasted boat?'

'Look on it as repaying a debt, Rebecca. You desert me for two years, and you smash up my boat.' The blandness in his voice mocked her anger. 'Playing the devoted wife to clinch my business deal is the least you can do, my darling.'

She was quivering with rage. Beginning to push

her chair back, she found herself pinned to her seat. Matt's hard fingers restrained her with insulting ease.

'No, you don't,' he warned softly. 'You're not walking out on me again, Becky.'

'Now that I'm not confined to the prison of a thirty-foot yacht, I can walk out on you whenever I like, Matt,' she informed him frigidly. 'And even if out of a sense of—of guilt...I consented to come and *pose* as your devoted wife in Athens, how could you be sure your precious business deal wouldn't go the same way as the boat?'

'Accidental sabotage? Or deliberate?' His silky tone made her blood run cold.

She clenched her fists, trying to wrench free of his grip.

'I didn't deliberately crash your boat,' she muttered angrily.

'While we're in Athens, I'd also like to take the opportunity to discuss some plans with you,' he continued, as if she hadn't spoken. 'Plans for investment in Sofie and Richard's restaurant business.'

She felt her jaw drop involuntarily. Gathering her wits, she glared at him in accusing disbelief.

'Are you *blackmailing* me, Matt?'

'With your narrow, suspicious little mind, I thought you might see it that way,' he countered lightly. Releasing her wrists, he leaned back lazily, his eyes very piercing under heavy lids. 'Relax, my darling, it won't be so bad. A chance to do some heavy-duty clothes shopping, dress up at night, dazzle my business colleagues and their wives, and safeguard Sofie and Richard's restaurant into the bargain. What could be fairer than that?'

'What kind of friend are you to Richard and Sofie,' she spat shakily, 'if you can't just help them for the sake of friendship alone?'

'Everyone needs some kind of return on their investments, Becky.'

'You really are the most...' Words failed her. 'I knew you were ruthless and selfish, Matt. But I didn't realise just how *manipulative* you were!'

'Years of practice.' Their coffees arrived, and he requested the bill, his eyes glinting with a triumph which made her want to attack him physically.

'We'll go across to Athens tonight. And whether you like it or not, Becky, it's time you fully appreciated the influence you have over my life. Thanks to you, my lifestyle of two years back—like my wife—vanished without trace. Now here you are, magically helping me to set up my new lifestyle.' The deep voice held a derisive hint of bitterness which shook her to the core as he added softly, 'What a truly powerful lady you are, Mrs Hawke.'

'I don't understand,' she said slowly, cautiously opening one of the mountain of carrier-bags and holding a forest-green silk dress against her. She was in the sumptuous grey and crimson splendour of their hotel suite, with Matt lazily sprawled on a Lloyd Loom sofa by the French doors on to the balcony, a gin and tonic on the table beside him.

He was bathed and changed for dinner, devastating in cream dinner-jacket and silk shirt, black trousers and bow-tie. A subtle trace of the spicy musk aftershave that Matt always used lingered in the air, assaulting her senses, reminding her of the past.

Below them was Syntagma Square, in the heart of the city. Even with the doors closed, and the air-conditioning controlling the temperature in the room, the noise and heat of the city floated up to them in almost tangible waves. 'What are you really getting out of this, Matt?'

'A beautiful, immaculately dressed *wife*, to accompany me to dinner?' The cool amusement in his voice made her heart thud with anger.

'Of course. Silly me.' She nodded mockingly. She'd just come out of the bathroom, clad in an ivory towelling robe and nothing else apart from a triangle of white silk panties. 'For a minute there, I was trying to work out why you've just spent all this money on clothes for me! If you'll excuse me, I'll go and get dressed.'

'Just a minute.' Matt's deep voice held an ominously silken note of command. 'Devoted wives don't scurry off to the bathroom to get dressed, Becky. Especially when their husbands have just lavished thousands of drachmas on a new wardrobe for them.'

Trembling, she stood her ground. She would *not* let him see how deeply his little power games were hurting her, and she would not be intimidated. She'd made these resolutions when she'd agreed to come to Athens and play Matt's twisted charade of happily married couples. Now, she forced herself to turn and meet his glittering, mocking gaze.

'Oh, I *see*,' she murmured, drawing a shaky breath. 'You want a *peep* show, do you, darling?'

'Naturally. A husband is entitled to watch his wife getting dressed, wouldn't you agree?'

'I don't recall it forming part of the marriage vows,' she countered acidly, 'but if that's the way you need to get your perverted kicks, who am I to argue?'

With a wildly kicking pulse-rate, she shrugged off the robe with careless languor, and turned her back on him. There was a long mirror in the door of the dark carved wardrobe. She could see herself, slim and high-breasted, the silk panties cut revealingly high on the hip, and she could see Matt behind her, sitting like an arrogant judge, his long legs stretched in front of him.

It was no good, she couldn't prevent the rush of colour to her neck and face. Matt's darkly brooding presence by the window and the veiled expression in his eyes were totally unnerving. With shaking

hands she sought the matching, lace-trimmed white
silk bra, and slipped it on. The fastening refused to
co-operate. She was shaking so much that she was
in danger of giving herself away completely. How
could she feign bored uninterest if she was trembling
all over?

'Would you like some help?' The toneless murmur made her tense defensively.

'No, I'm quite capable of getting dressed without
help,' she managed stiffly, clipping the lacy white
suspender belt round her narrow waist and sitting
down on the bed to gather one fine grey silk stocking in her hands before hooking it over her toes.
When both stockings were fastened she stood up
again, ignoring him completely, her cheeks on fire.

'Wear the emerald and silver earrings with that
dress,' he advised coolly. She'd shrugged the dark
green silk over her head and wriggled the wrap-over
bodice to fit snugly. She did the necessary contortion
to fasten the back zip, determined not to ask Matt
for help.

The skirt was full, hanging in elegant folds to
calf-length. With short, floppy, 'Peter Pan' sleeves,
and a subtle darker green embroidery at neck and
hem, it was a dreamy, gorgeous dress, which made
her feel floaty, feminine and disturbingly vulnerable.

'Whatever you say,' she began calmly, then
stopped, swivelling to face him. She was so angry,
suddenly, that she couldn't hide it any longer. 'Do

you imagine that treating me like—like some cheap *whore* you've paid to entertain you is going to make me *love* you again, Matt?'

Matt's face was implacable. His features could have been carved in granite.

'Are you saying you loved me once?' His voice was grimly devoid of emotion. He didn't move a muscle, but his eyes held her rooted to the spot.

'You know I did!' Her throat was so tight that her voice sounded choked and faint. 'I was so in love with you, I couldn't even think straight!'

Matt stood up in a fluid determined motion. She had to grit her teeth to stand her ground as he walked across the bedroom towards her.

'That's not the way it seemed to me,' he said quietly. He reached out to take her chin between his thumb and forefinger, twisting her face up to scan the expression in her wide hazel eyes. 'It seemed to me that our marriage was a sham—convenient when you were pregnant, an obstacle to your career and your studies when you weren't. Your friend Ted Whiteman filled me in on how much you resented giving up your freedom, Becky. Su-Lin was just an excuse, wasn't she? An excuse to justify walking out on me?'

She could hardly breathe. The touch of his fingers, his nearness, the words he was saying—everything was combining to make her feel sick with disbelief.

'If you believe that...' she managed unsteadily.

'If you think I behaved like that, why on earth are you bothering with this stupid charade tonight?'

'I always enjoyed charades.' He let go of her chin, slid his fingers up the tender underside of her jaw, and circled the delicate hollow of her ear. His touch sent a frisson of reaction along her nerve-ends. 'And maybe I'm a masochist.'

'A sadist more likely…' She tried to inject cool cynicism into her tone, but it came out on a croaky tremble.

Abruptly, with suppressed ferocity, Matt bent and kissed her, catching hold of the other side of her head, trapping her there while he plundered her mouth hungrily, punishingly.

There were tears in her eyes when he stopped.

'Matt…*don't*,' she choked thickly. 'Don't hate me, I can't bear it.'

'Sweet *hell*, Becky…' In a muted flurry of need, she was crushed against him. The heat and the physical hunger threatened to soar totally out of control. Her dress was half off, the back zip down and her whole body flushed with response, when the telephone buzzed.

Matt went very still, a shudder jolting through him. He rested his forehead against hers, his breathing shallow. He let her go and grabbed the receiver. When he dropped it back, she'd subsided on to the end of the bed, clutching her dress against her.

'That was Reception. Alexis and his wife are downstairs waiting for us.'

She met his eyes. The electricity charging the air between them was still there. She was tense all over.

'In that case,' she managed stiffly, 'unless you want to flaunt your wife's image as loose and wanton, you'd better do my zip up for me.'

Matt's warm fingers slid all the way up her spine as he zipped the dress. She closed her eyes, and prayed for self-control. The evening ahead sounded fraught enough, without fighting this melting weakness whenever Matt looked at her, or touched her.

Alexis and his wife were charming. She remembered him, vaguely, as one of the two Greek businessmen who'd been with Matt that night at the Old Mill Restaurant, at the beginning of their roller-coaster affair which had led to their current dismal battleground.

'The sorrel soup,' Alexis laughed, shaking her hand with such a twinkle in his eye that she had to laugh back. 'How could I forget?'

'Chivalry decrees that you do now,' said his wife Elisavet who, dark and graceful, gave him a repressive glance as they braved the oven-hot night outside the hotel and found a taxi. They drove to meet the rest of the party at a nightclub in the Kolonaki, a buzzing, fashionable area of the city below the soaring hill of Mount Likavetos.

The roar and chaos of the city distracted Becky from the tension with Matt. Athens seemed to thrive on its own unbearable heat. Glittering with lights and thronging with people, the city was shabbily glamorous, sprawled beneath the awesome grandeur of the Acropolis, with the temperatures high enough to fry eggs on the crowded pavements.

'If it wasn't for business, I wouldn't be here. I hate the place in summer,' Matt confided with a grin as they walked into the air-conditioned club. 'Too hot. But at least I've got your arctic glances to cool me down.'

The ruthless taunt in his eyes was only partly masked by the smile on his lips.

'Of course, business must come first,' she countered, her smile coldly hostile.

Elisavet steered her off to where the other couples sat and introduced her with such warmth that she felt, despite herself, a hidden glow of confused pride. These people were welcoming her, treating her like a VIP simply because she was Matt Hawke's wife. The sensation, to her surprise, was far from unpleasant. No amount of self-mocking counselling seemed to alter this fact.

Which made it all a thousand times worse, she reflected miserably, smiling and chatting as they looked at the menu, enjoying the sophisticated blend of business, gossip and political comment flowing to and fro between the assembled company.

Laughing at something Elisavet said, she caught Matt's lidded eyes on her. Her fingers stilled on the stem of her aperitif glass.

They were seated at their table, awaiting the arrival of one more couple before ordering their meals. Around them was the relaxed glamour of the restaurant area of the club, laid out on a higher level than the intimate-looking dance floor.

The muted colour scheme was dark green and plum, romantically lit, glittering with candlelight, dotted with huge green plants and scented flowers. The place was humming with cosmopolitan life— the men in dinner-jackets, the women in jewel-coloured dresses, a discreet gleam of gold at their throats and ears—but somehow the only reality was Matt's dark blue gaze. Meeting it was like submerging in shadows, sinking into deep water. She couldn't tear her eyes away...

Alexis was saying something which grabbed her attention suddenly. Abruptly she dragged her mesmerised eyes from Matt's, focusing on the Greek man's face.

'But you say the boat *is* repairable?' he was finishing, his expression wryly amused.

'So the boatyard tells me,' Matt drawled, with a laugh, 'though I doubt if I'll be doing any sailing in her again this summer.'

Becky felt her neck go hot as she tuned into their conversation.

'*How* did you say the accident happened again?' Alexis was probing, a strong trace of merciless teasing in his voice which made her shrivel inside.

'Well, now…' She was holding her breath, she realised, rigid with apprehension. The pause seemed to go on forever, but Matt's harsh features were blandly merciless as she risked a glance at him. 'How *did* it happen, Becky?'

Appalled, she stared at him with widening eyes. Opening her mouth, she tried to formulate a suitable reply. She could say, Matt kidnapped me and I was trying to escape, but not only would that sound hilariously unbelievable, it wouldn't fit in terribly well with her role as the devoted little wife tonight. It would hardly serve to boost Matt's image for his new business partners, would it? Panic whirled in her head.

So much for her poised sophistication in the new dress and expensive jewellery that Matt had paid for. She'd turned scarlet. She wished the floor would open and swallow her. The silence hung just long enough to turn heads, raise a few amused eyebrows.

'It was entirely my fault.' Matt's narrowed blue eyes gleamed with cruel amusement as he smoothly rescued her. His tone was calmly self-mocking. 'I didn't secure a safe anchorage. The *meltemi* blew up. I was on the beach with Becky. My mind was on other things…'

'Ah…' The male exchange of glances as old as

time, and chauvinistically insulting, Becky thought furiously. But at least she was off the hook. '*Now* I understand!' Alexis finished up, his dark eyes appreciative as he swept them over Becky's slender curves and over-bright eyes. 'With such a distraction, accidents could happen all the time.'

'When you have quite finished embarrassing Becky,' Elisavet intervened lightly, her dark eyes sympathetic at Becky's mortified appearance, 'the Changs have just arrived.'

Becky followed Elisavet's gaze. At the entrance to the restaurant a short, distinguished-looking grey-haired man, with unmistakably Chinese features, was being greeted by the head waiter and pointed in the direction of their table.

At his side walked a girl of such stunning oriental beauty that even the sophisticated Athenians turned their heads to stare. Petite, curvaceous but perfectly proportioned, in a gold-embroidered high-necked sheath, her shining jet-black hair hanging almost to her waist, she glowed like a softly ripe peach at her father's side.

With a mounting sense of bitter disbelief, Becky felt her heart stop, then kick into horrified thudding. Su-Lin was gliding towards them, pink mouth curved in a seductive smile, her almond-shaped eyes trained exclusively on Matt...

CHAPTER EIGHT

THE meal passed in a kind of vacuum—a blur of delicious food, expensive wine and polished conversation in which Becky endeavoured to participate without consciously knowing how.

It was like a nasty dream, she thought sickly. Like a replay of the past, except that the past crises over Su-Lin had taken place at a distance from her, whereas the present situation was being thrust at her head-on.

She wanted to run away. She wanted to get up and march out of the darkly intimate club, escape into the bustle and anonymity of Athens at night, and run and run until she never had to see Matt again.

But Matt seemed to be watching her whenever she risked a glance at him. His gaze seemed to remind her silently of her promise. It was an amused, goading look which almost seemed to dare her to walk out on him...

Would he *really* decide against funding Sofie's and Richard's business if she let him down tonight? It was too great a risk to take. Sofie might be sitting exasperatingly on the fence over the feud with Matt, but she'd helped her in so many ways since their parents had died. If tonight's sacrifice repaid a little of her kindness it would be worth it, wouldn't it?

Hardly trusting herself, she averted her eyes from that narrowed blue gaze. She doubted if she could have brought herself to make civil conversation with him, whatever her so-called duties tonight, but fortunately he was talking to either Alexis or Kenneth Chang most of the time.

The Changs appeared to have hotel and shipping links with the Greek consortium, and were moving the base for some of their interests from Hong Kong to Athens. The common denominator seemed to be Matt's dealings with both parties. Further than that, she neither concentrated nor cared.

'So...you are *still* Matt's wife?' Su-Lin's soft voice was for Becky's ears only, but the delicate trace of hatred was unmistakable. The meal was over and some colourful Greek dancers had appeared on the dance-floor to hold everyone spellbound. The party had moved down to sit and have coffee in a more relaxed area, nearer the dance-floor and the discreetly lit bar, and the dark girl had slid into the seat nearest to Becky.

Her stomach contracting, she turned level hazel eyes on Su-Lin.

'Yes, I am.' She forced a calm smile. She was aware that Matt was watching them lazily, leaning against the bar while Alexis talked to him animatedly. Elisavet was glancing at her, dark eyes curious. She felt as if she was on a tightrope; one slip and she'd crash down, bringing Matt's whole sick charade with her.

'For how much longer, I wonder?' Su-Lin's eyes were dark as sloes in the exquisite oval of her face.

Becky gave a shaky shrug. 'The marriage vows say "Till death us do part", don't they?'

'Indeed they do,' Matt's voice cut in drily. Without her noticing, he'd come to lean on the back of her chair. She nearly dropped her coffee. The small gold cup wobbled precariously. She put it down on the low glass table with a shaky clatter. 'I'm glad you've met Su-Lin, Becky. Though I'm not sure you'll find that you have a great deal in common.' There was an edge of steel in his tone.

Becky stared up at him. The dark face looked even more cynical than normal. The mesmerising gaze was lidded. Deep vertical furrows ran from the sides of his nose to the corners of his mouth. He looked like an implacable stranger and her whole body clenched with angry tension.

Su-Lin rose gracefully to her feet, flicking a winsome gaze at Matt from beneath long, silken lashes.

'Matt, darling,' she murmured sensuously, 'it's lovely seeing you again tonight. How long are you staying in Athens?'

'Just long enough to wrap up this deal,' he said

smoothly. 'Becky and I are keen to get back to the fresher air of the islands, aren't we, sweetheart?'

Su-Lin's expression tautened. Becky caught her breath. Was this the *real* reason why Matt had insisted that she come with him to Athens? To present the image of a patched-up marriage as a neat way of extricating himself from his affair with Su-Lin? And without alienating her wealthy father?

She'd never felt more used, more manipulated.

She stood up stiffly, fumbling for her small black velvet evening-bag. Her heart was hammering like a piston. Keeping her churning emotions under control was draining, exhausting. To hell with Matt and his scheming; he'd gone too far. The pain of having Su-Lin paraded under her nose, cold-bloodedly thrust upon her, was too much.

'Would you excuse me…?' she began bitterly. 'I need some fresh air right *now*—'

'I understand,' Su-Lin cut in quickly, her high voice sharp with malice. 'Clinging on to a sham marriage can be so stifling, I should imagine.'

'Who said anything about a sham?' Matt snaked out his hand and caught Becky's arm, stopping her in her tracks. 'Ours is the real thing, isn't it, sweetheart?'

'Matt…I…'

'After two years' separation?' Su-Lin hissed. Her dark eyes were liquid with fury. 'I don't think you can want each other so very much!'

'But I do want my wife. Very much.' The quiet
assertion held such grim certainty that Becky felt a
great wash of heat, mounting and receding in her
face. A breathless stillness enveloped her in the steel
grip of Matt's fingers. What a convincing fraud he
was! How could he be so…*treacherous*? How could
he use people so ruthlessly? In spite of everything,
in spite of the glitter of hatred and pain in Su-Lin's
eyes, she almost felt sorry for the other girl.

Her surroundings receded, became unreal. The
bouzouki and violin music on the dance-floor, the
sensual rhythm of the dancers as they twisted,
turned, dipped and swayed in their colourful, tradi-
tional costumes, the muted hubbub of talk and
laughter in the club—nothing seemed real any more.
Just Matt, and the hard glitter in his eyes as they
locked with hers.

'I can see that you and Su-Lin have a lot to talk
about,' she managed frigidly. Stepping sideways,
she managed to escape Matt's hold. 'And I've
played enough games for one night.'

Dimly aware that Alexis and Elisavet were ob-
serving the small scene, she made desperately for
the door. She no longer cared if her abrupt departure
embarrassed Matt's business interests. Even safe-
guarding Sofie's future became secondary to the
need to escape this unbearable pain. She couldn't
stay a second longer.

She struck out blindly from the nightclub's discreet exit, and met the blast of warm air of the Athens summer evening. She was crying, she realised distantly. Bars and elegant, glittering cafés lined the street, the haunting minor-key strains of Greek music floating from one of them.

There was a stall selling barbecued corn on the cob at the corner; the sweet aroma wafted at her as she pushed by. She didn't know where she was heading. The tears were blurring her vision. Crying over Matt was something she'd thought she'd finished months ago. Why, oh, why did he have to come back like this and churn up the dust and wreckage of their marriage? Why did he have to be such a *perfidious*, self-centred con-man?

'Becky...*Becky*!'

He was following her. A quick glance over her shoulder showed Matt's broad-shouldered figure, with its athletic lope, swiftly gaining on her. Idiotically she broke into a run, uncaring of how silly she must look in her evening dress and low-heeled black suede court shoes. A few seconds later he'd reached her side and caught hold of her, swinging her to a shuddering halt.

'We're not exactly dressed for jogging,' he quipped tersely. His cream dinner-jacket had flapped open, and his bow-tie had been tugged loose. He looked very dark, and forbidding as he glared down at her. 'And when are you going to stop throwing in the goddammed towel and running away when things don't go just the way you think they should?'

'*Typical*!' she hurled at him, out of breath. 'It's always my fault, isn't it? You—you blackmail me into this stupid pretence of being happily married, you treat me like some hired *prostitute*, you conveniently forget to tell me that your *mistress* is coming to dinner...'

They'd stopped by a pavement café full of elegant-looking people sitting talking and sipping drinks under the bright awnings, or lazily watching the world go by. Becky sensed that she and Matt were becoming the focus of intense curiosity. She stiffened, tried to wriggle free, but Matt was holding her upper arm in a vice-like grip.

'Would you have come if I'd told you?'

'I don't know! I care about Sofie. But maybe even the fate of my sister's business wouldn't have seemed worth the humiliation.'

Matt's eyes were shadowed, but a quirk of his lips signalled grim humour. 'Ah, yes. My scurrilous blackmail?'

'You think you're so powerful, so clever! I just want you out of my life, and all I get is harrassment and—'

'Admit it, you came with me to Athens because you wanted to, Becky.'

'You're so *arrogant*! Matt, *hating* you just isn't strong enough...'

'Let's get out of here,' he murmured, bleak amusement in his eyes. She glanced vaguely round them. Their audience now comprised nearly all of the café's clientele. 'We'll take the funicular railway up Mount Likavetos,' he added tersely, steering her away from the curious eyes. 'There's a place up there we can talk.'

In tense silence she sat beside him as the railway rose steeply, lifting them higher and higher through the star-sprinkled sky. At the top, she caught her breath involuntarily at the view from the cosily lit open-air café. In spite of her anguish, the sight spread beneath her was spectacular. The mountain dwarfed even the Acropolis in all its timeless beauty. Far down in the valley, the lights of Athens pulsed like a million tiny glow-worms. There was even the faintest suggestion of a breeze to lighten the intense heat of the night.

'Coffee?' Matt queried bluntly. 'Or something stronger?'

'I'm not sure I want anything...' She met his eyes across the glass-topped table, hardly conscious of the hovering waiter.

'Two brandies,' he ordered quietly, dismissing the waiter before she could argue.

'You think you're some kind of—of god, don't you?' she bit out furiously. 'Deciding, arranging, *using* people...'

'I haven't used you, Becky.'

'You tricked me into that sailing trip. You're supposedly *using* me tonight as some kind of window-dressing for your business deal. You spring Su-Lin on me without a word of warning... I could kill you.'

'No, you couldn't.' His wryly humorous voice made everything ten times more infuriating. 'You're much too sweet-natured to kill anything, my darling.'

'Don't *patronise* me! I am *not* your darling!' she flung at him passionately.

'And Su-Lin is not my mistress.'

There was a fraught pause. She dashed a shaky hand over her eyes, striving for control. 'You expect me to believe that?'

Matt's powerful shoulders lifted in a shrug. His jaw was taut as he watched her steadily.

'On past experience, I doubt if I've a hope in hell,' he agreed bleakly.

She opened her mouth to speak, then stopped. Her brain felt as if it had switched on to overload. 'Su-Lin certainly seems to think she is,' she managed quietly.

'Su-Lin has always had a problem with the truth. And our problem is that paranoid jealousy and happy marriages don't go together, do they?'

She was hugging her arms round herself, despite the muggy warmth of the night. There was a heady scent of pines, the shrill of a thousand cicadas on the velvet darkness of the hillside. A couple strolled past the tables, arms round each other, heads bent in soft conversation. Lovers in the moonlight, she thought miserably. In different circumstances Athens would be a good city for lovers—the heat, the relaxed warmth of the Greeks themselves...

'Jealousy?' she said at last. 'That's only a tiny bit of what went wrong, isn't it? At least... At least jealousy is an active, positive emotion. It shows someone *cares*.'

Their brandies arrived. She stared at hers mutinously for a while, then took a sip. The strong liquid burned all the way down to her stomach, reviving her nerves a little.

'If you're saying I didn't care about you, you're wrong,' Matt told her softly. He was watching her over the globe of golden candlelight on their table. His gaze was disturbingly hard to interpret.

She closed her eyes. She had to get her thoughts straight. She had to make some sense of her feelings.

'Matt, you can't just *say* that.' She spoke with elaborate care. Her heart was thudding; her throat felt dry. 'You need to show it. Don't you see? When I needed you—really needed you—you weren't there. You were on the next plane out of town.'

'I know.'

She stared at him blankly.

'Actions speak louder than words, you mean?' he

went on, his voice suddenly grimmer. 'God, Becky, do you think I don't know that I let you down?'

His taut admission made her heart quiver into brief stillness, before thumping harder.

'Well, then…' A glimpse of the harsh lines of his face made her feel hot all over. This was unnerving. Matt being arrogant and manipulative, she was accustomed to; Matt being wryly honest and disarmingly humble, she wasn't at all sure she could handle with any degree of poise.

'I told you, on the beach at Skyros,' he went on doggedly, 'I wasn't ready for commitment.' His brief smile was bleak. 'If you want the truth, Becky, it scared the hell out of me.'

'What? Knowing that I was madly in love with you?' Her bitterness made him flinch slightly.

'Not knowing if you thought you'd made a big mistake,' he said quietly. 'Wondering if Ted Whiteman was right—if I'd screwed up your life for you by getting you pregnant.'

'Just a minute. Will you stop bringing Ted Whiteman into this? He was just a—a friend…'

She had a mental picture of Ted—crinkly brown eyes, rather arty long brown hair, flowing designer clothes. As head of the model agency that had taken her on as a student he'd shown flattering disappointment at her decision to quit completely. But then, after she'd lost the baby, he'd just been a kind friend. In Matt's frequent, prolonged absences abroad he'd called her, taken her to dinner a couple of times, been *supportive* just when she'd most needed someone to be supportive...

'At least he came round and spent some time with me after I had the miscarriage, which is more than you did!'

'Quite.' Matt's tone was lethally sarcastic. 'I just met you, got you pregnant and married you. What more did you want?'

There was a tight ball of pain and anger somewhere in the region of her solar plexus.

'You didn't *get* me pregnant,' she corrected him huskily. 'It takes two to make a baby, Matt. And—and finding out that I was pregnant was the—the most...the best thing that had ever happened to me...'

'And then suddenly you weren't pregnant,' he agreed drily. With a jerk, he drank some of his brandy. He put the glass down on the table with a click of suppressed violence. There was a note in his voice that she didn't understand. 'And so the best thing had gone. Is that right?'

Emotion choked her, abruptly and overwhelmingly. Her throat felt so full up that she could hardly speak.

'Matt...it seems to me that I can't win this argument. If I tell you I loved you, you bring Ted Whiteman into it. If I say that I was overjoyed about having a baby, you accuse me of only marrying you because my baby needed a father.

'What you don't seem to grasp, in your pigheaded arrogance, is that when I needed you, when I desperately needed you there for me, you backed off. You went abroad. You stayed away. You went to nightclubs in Hong Kong with Su-Lin and got your picture in the social columns. What kind of a caring, supportive husband behaves like that?'

'One who's hurting as much as his wife.'

She risked a jerky look at him. She couldn't trust him, she told herself warily. This new hint of frankness was just another of Matt Hawke's amazing repertoire of psychological games. The man was obsessed with keeping control. If one avenue appeared to be closed to him he found another, as rapidly as a computer analysed data.

'You're trying to tell me that losing the baby hurt you as much as it hurt me?'

'I can't answer that.' His gaze was grimly resigned. He turned his head away, gazing down over the spangled jewels of Athens far below.

His voice was low when he said, 'What I'm trying to tell you, Becky, is that I wanted our baby. I really wanted it. Until you surprised me with it, I admit that I hadn't given the idea of fatherhood any thought at all. But then it seemed like a great idea— getting married, starting a family suddenly seemed a great idea. Then you had the miscarriage, and you just seemed to fall apart. All I could think of was that you didn't seem to want me around. You shut me out...'

'I didn't mean to,' she said tightly. Matt was still looking away from her. She dropped her eyes to her brandy-glass in case he suddenly looked back at her. She didn't trust herself now; she didn't want him to read her eyes. 'Matt, I felt devastated. My—my hormones were messed up. You seemed distant suddenly. It felt like a—a wedge between us. An invisible wedge. Do you understand?'

He expelled his breath slowly. There was a long silence.

'When I was twelve, my mother left my father,' he told her quietly. 'He couldn't cope at all. He fell apart. I vowed that I'd never let a woman do that to me. I think I felt...you were leaving me...mentally.' He grinned bleakly as he glanced round at her. 'Does that sound like psycho-babble?'

She realised suddenly that this was the first time he'd told her himself about his mother. Sofie had supplied her with the information, but somehow they'd never got round to talking to each other about their pasts. Was it because there'd always been too much drama going on in the present? Their affair had been rapid, passionate and, when she looked back now, regrettably superficial. A forced relationship, she realised sadly. Forced by her discovery of the pregnancy, Matt's insistence on marriage...

She swallowed the lump of pain in her throat. Now wasn't the time to let sympathy for Matt well up and blind her to the truth. It was too late.

'So you left me, instead?'

'I didn't leave you, Becky. I had to travel abroad on business. You're the one who left,' he said flatly. His eyes were harder, his expression so hostile that she caught her breath with a shaky gasp. Her emotions were in turmoil. She could hardly remember what they'd said. That sensation of floating apart was back so strongly that she could almost feel the gulf widening between them.

'I left you...because there was nothing else for me to do.' She shivered as she said it. It sounded so bleak, so final. It seemed to herald the imminence of their divorce as clearly as a trumpet sounding. Why did her heart feel as if it was splitting open?

'And now, here we are again,' he murmured. His eyes were shuttered as he looked at her white face. 'Still causing each other as much pain as before.'

'Oh, no,' she said quickly. She was shaking her head with an involuntary vehemence, her palms damp as all her defences flew into position. 'No, Matt. If I still cared for you, you'd be hurting me now, playing your little power games. But I don't...'

'You don't?' His smile was hard, lacking any humour at all.

'No.' She pressed on with determination. 'This last two years, I've—I've matured a lot. I'll never let another relationship threaten me the way ours did. I'll never play the pawn in your narrow-minded, ambitious world again.'

There was another charged silence. His face was a hard mask.

'Quite,' he said expressionlessly. 'Still, my little power games have, hopefully, borne fruit. As of tonight, unless your dramatic departure has scotched the deal, I've set myself up with a lucrative part-time consultancy with Alexis and his group. And if I decide on some investment in the Old Mill Restaurant, I think my new lifestyle will have enough to keep my narrow, ambitious mind ticking over. Shall we go, Mrs Hawke?'

He didn't touch her as they walked to the funicular. She gripped her bag under her arm, keeping the other hand clenched at her side. The six inches separating her from Matt seemed a mile wide. Their marriage was dead, she told herself ruthlessly. This desolate longing was just a natural, passing reaction to the inevitability of change, of letting go...

'*If* you decide on investment in the Old Mill?' she queried abruptly. They were walking back to their hotel by the time she'd found the strength to query his last cryptic comment. 'You said that if I came to Athens with you for this business dinner you'd definitely help Sofie and Richard.'

'True. But that was dependent on your posing convincingly as my devoted wife, my darling.' The blue gaze glinted dangerously. 'Alexis and Elisavet were a little surprised to see you dashing out of the nightclub as if pursued by demons.'

'So I was supposed to just sit there and—and put up with Su-Lin's taunts? And now you're accusing me of ruining your precious deal?' she demanded, glaring at him in outrage. 'My God, Matt, you're really pushing your luck!'

'Relax,' he soothed infuriatingly. 'Stop jumping to conclusions. That's your biggest fault, Mrs Hawke—jumping to conclusions.'

She drew a long, steadying breath. She had to stop letting him rile her; she rose to the bait every time. What pleasure he must be deriving from teasing and taunting her when she was such easy game.

'The conclusion was forced on me,' she said quietly. 'Just like the realisation that the reason you married me, and not Su-Lin, was because I was expecting your baby.'

'Here we go again. I only married you because I got you pregnant.' Matt glanced down at her as they walked, his eyes ominously bland.

'Stop being so patronising,' she said hotly. 'And stop talking as if you were the sole participant!'

He smiled thinly.

'Speaking of getting you pregnant, Mrs Hawke, is there any chance that history might repeat itself after this last couple of days?'

'No,' she managed, with as much dignity as she

could muster. 'If you think I'd leave myself open to that mistake again, you really don't think much of my intellect!'

She couldn't tell if his expression was relieved or disappointed. It was like having a conversation with a masked bandit, she thought furiously.

'So you're on the Pill?' His tone was silken with mockery.

'Exactly... Of course I am—' She broke off abruptly.

They'd reached a busy crossroads, and Matt reached out his arm to stop her from stepping blindly into the road in front of a madly speeding taxi. A horn blared as the car shot past them.

She was hot in the face as he hauled her to safety. But realisation had just hit her, with the force of a body blow. A sick, sinking sense of dismay was spreading from her throat, down through her chest, and into her stomach.

She had taken the Pill, true. On a regualr basis. But she hadn't done so for some time. And the flare of angry passion between them had apparently deadened her brain to such mundane technicalities.

Could she possibly have conceived, during one of those violent lapses in self-control? History repeating itself? Matt's heartless taunt echoed round and round in her head. She shivered, in spite of the warmth.

'So the good old contraceptive pill has been a

necessary precaution in your lifestyle since you walked out on me?' Matt was now steering her across the road with proprietorial care. She flinched in his grip. She couldn't think of any reply.

His gaze was probingly intent on her tense face as they reached the far side. 'What's the matter, Becky? Have you just remembered something?'

Her cheeks grew even hotter at the remorseless mockery in his tone. He knew... He'd known all along, of course. How could she have been so... *stupid*? She'd been reeling in her shocked, emotional turmoil—practical considerations had totally eluded her. But Matt had known...

'I know what you're trying to do, Matt,' she said shakily, 'but you're not going to succeed.'

'You mean it's out of line to talk about your other relationships since you left me? It's OK for you to accuse me of adultery,' he mused lightly, 'but not for me to accuse you?'

He was deliberately misunderstanding her, she knew. Through clenched teeth, she said, 'Just to put the record straight, I've never committed *adultery*— not with Ted Whiteman, not with *anyone*! But that's not what I meant at all.' Her voice was cracking slightly as she shuddered with angry emotion. 'I meant that if you imagine that you can continue to manipulate me, to—to keep me as one of your *possessions* by getting me pregnant again, think again.'

They'd reached the entrance of their hotel, and

she glanced at him quickly, her eyes very bright with unshed tears. 'And if by any chance I *have* conceived during this last couple of days, I'll do everything I can to make sure you never have anything to do with my baby, Matt!'

CHAPTER NINE

'ARE you saying—' Matt's voice was ruthlessly triumphant as they stood in the silence of the hotel lift
'—that there's a chance you might be pregnant
again?'

Becky winced. They weren't alone in the lift.
Apart from the uniformed lift-boy there were two
elegantly dressed American ladies, whose conversation had meaningfully ceased after Matt's cool
question.

The tension was almost tangible.

'That *is* an interesting thought,' he persisted
softly. The wicked glint in his eyes made her simmer
with fury. The back wall of the lift was mirrored.
She glimpsed their images—her own tautly pale, all
eyes and lips in the white of her face, Matt's darkly
amused, his features swarthily attractive against the
contrast of his dinner-jacket. The lift-boy looked
professionally expressionless. The well-dressed
ladies were gazing at the dark blue carpet floor.

'How you can...*crow* like this, when you could
be responsible for getting me pregnant against my

wishes…!' She couldn't help it—the whispered accusation burst out, her temper erupting involuntarily.

'I thought ''getting'' you pregnant was the wrong phrase?' he teased mercilessly. '''It takes two to make a baby,'' you said earlier.'

'It takes two people who love each other and who *want* to make a baby.'

'Wrong again, sweetheart. Our first jackpot had plenty of love, but we didn't set out to make a baby, did we?'

The lift had stopped, and their fellow guests left with evident reluctance. Becky felt almost feverish with fury. Their suite was on the top floor. She bit her lip until the deadpan lift-boy had disappeared with the lift, and they were inside their room.

Rounding on him, she lifted her hands in small fists to fend him off. She was trembling all over with rage.

'This time there was no love at all. And I should think it's *highly* unlikely that I could conceive after just…just…'

'Just doing what we did on the beach?' His wryly tilted eyebrow brought a flood of heat to her face. 'I'd say we took all the requisite steps involved in the baby-making process, sweetheart, wouldn't you?'

'Having your baby is the *last* thing I'd ever contemplate doing again,' she forged on hoarsely, hating him for his cool mockery. 'And if I did find I was pregnant again it would be all your fault!'

'I don't recall forcing you,' he mused ruthlessly. 'Are you saying I forced you?'

'You *kidnapped* me, goddammit!'

'Hush, Becky. Too much temper could raise your blood pressure; very bad in the early stages of pregnancy…'

His laconic teasing was the final straw. With a hoarse sob, she flew at him, anger scything through her uncontrollably. He caught her against the warmth of his chest, trapping her arms, pinning her there forcibly. The lean wall of muscle seemed to burn her through the fine silk of his shirt. 'Let's go to bed and talk about this, shall we?'

She freed herself just enough to stare incredulously into his face. There was that dangerous gleam in his eyes again. Crimes of passion suddenly seemed only too understandable; she had a brief, gratifying image of strangling Matt with her bare hands. Then the image crumbled into holding him in her arms, kissing him with all the suppressed, resentful desire he could still whip up inside her with a single glance. She caught her breath on a sob.

'Go to *bed*? If you *touch* me tonight, I'll—I'll ring the police and claim marital rape!'

'Hey, loosen up,' he teased huskily. 'It's not my fault you've got a bad memory, is it?'

The cool gleam of humour in his eyes was devastating. She wanted to hit him again. She pushed herself free of him, and went out on to the balcony. She stood there trembling, gripping the rail with shaky tension.

'Face it, Becky, maybe what happened on the beach on Skyros would have happened anyway. Maybe it wasn't something we had a lot of control over?'

Matt's soft query caught her off guard. She glanced round slowly. He was standing a few feet behind her, hands in the pockets of his jacket, his features very hard.

Abruptly the fight drained out of her. Uncertainty took the place of anger. She shook her head slowly, confusion trickling through her. She felt almost dizzy with it... With a faint, self-deriding laugh, she thrust her fingers through the glossy bell of her hair, then let her hand fall limply to her side.

'I...I don't know,' she breathed at last. 'I honestly don't know.'

She met Matt's eyes. Was there just the merest trace of vulnerability lurking behind the lidded gaze? Or was it her imagination?

'That makes two of us.'

She drew a long breath.

'Even if that was the case...all it proves is that— that we're still sexually attracted.' She managed this with commendable coolness.

'True. That's one thing it proves.'

'Matt…' She gazed at him, a helpless feeling creeping through her. 'Matt, I'm so confused…'

'Did you bring your pills along with you on this trip?' he queried wryly.

She shook her head. Her lips twitched. Suddenly she was laughing, rather hysterically. She sat down abruptly on the chair by the window.

'The truth is that I stopped taking them while I took medication for that virus. Until you raised the subject at the café, I confess I'd forgotten all about the wretched things. They weren't something that played any meaningful role in my life, if you must know. They were… They were just a precaution, after what happened with you.'

'Becky…come here.'

The contained air about him had a mesmerising quality. Without conscious volition, she found herself standing up and slowly walking towards him.

'Will you change your mind about letting me touch you tonight?' His voice was a harsh caress. The suppressed ferocity of his desire was so potent that it reached her without his moving a muscle. 'I'm not too good at begging, sweetheart, but I need you. Right now I'm breaking up and falling apart with needing you.'

'Matt…I'm so afraid…' The catch in her voice turned the whisper into a croak.

'Of getting pregnant again?'

'No…of letting…of letting you close.'

'Becky...' He reached out, and took her into his arms. It was a convulsive jerk, trapping her there with suppressed violence. 'Becky, I'd rather cut my own throat than hurt you again.'

She could hardly breathe. Matt's hard nearness was triggering a hot, fiery reaction from her thighs to her breasts.

'Are you...?' She swallowed, and tried again. 'This isn't all about trying to start another baby, so that we'd feel morally tied together or something?'

His laugh was rough, his lips on her hair.

'You're so suspicious,' he murmured unsteadily. His voice had deepened, thickened. The heat between them was burning hotter, making her shake all over as he cupped her face, kissed her with rapid, branding, scorching kisses on her mouth, her cheeks, her neck.

'Haven't you worked it out yet?' he breathed, pushing her down on to the softness of the bed beside them, imprisoning her there with one hard thigh. 'All I want is you, Becky. Baby or no baby. If you want, I'll wear protection, tonight and every night. I'll personally supervise every goddamned pill you take in future. Just admit that you still feel something for me...'

'I do...still feel something for you.' Her eyes were pools of fiery gold-brown in her flushed face.

It was true, she realised with a surge of wary surrender. Whatever their future held, whatever game

Matt might be playing now, tonight the pretence was gone. She still loved him; she'd never stopped.

Her heart was beating so hard—so hard that she felt as if it might hammer a hole in her chest. Her stomach was liquid fire, aching with that familiar, uncontrollable response that Matt could always stir up inside her. She reached up a trembling hand, and touched the hard line of his jaw.

'And don't... Don't wear any protection,' she whispered unevenly, blushing deeply at the savage amusement in his eyes. 'For the moment at least you are still my legally wedded husband, aren't you?' She bit her lip on a tremulous smile, fresh warmth flooding her cheeks, and added huskily, 'And I want you... I want to feel *you* inside me.'

'Becky...oh, *God*, Becky...'

His last semblance of control was abruptly jettisoned. With a muffled expletive, he ripped off his bow-tie with one impatient, essentially masculine sweep, tearing off his jacket and shirt and then exploring the fastenings of her green silk dress. He drew it down over her arms with hands that shook with urgency and tension. Feeling almost disorientated, head spinning, she writhed with shivery impatience beneath him. He dispensed rapidly with the rest of his clothes, then began a slower, more sensual removal of her lacy bra. She sucked in her breath involuntarily as he unpeeled the fine white silk, revealing the high, pale globes of her breasts to his hungry gaze.

'You are so special.' He groaned the words with suppressed hunger, dropping his lips to her neck, to her collarbone, then lower, to mouth each taut, shivery nipple, moulding his hands around her breasts, smoothing and stroking the soft, sensitive undercurve with his thumbs. He caressed her breasts with such tender expertise that she felt as if they were the sole source of sensation in her body.

Then he moved his hands to her neck, traced the soft lobes of her ears, explored the delicate whorls with his fingers and his lips, until she cried out in choked need.

'Matt...please...' Every movement of his fingers was intensely erotic, unbearably arousing. She ached for him to touch her all over—to stroke his clever hands down to her stomach, to the hot, damp ache of liquid heat between her legs. She was on fire, burning, burning...

With a slight, choked laugh, half shy, half sensuous, she moved to grasp his shoulders, digging her fingernails into the taut silk of muscle there.

'Make love to me now,' she urged, on a small, hoarse plea. She felt wanton and profligate and wildly aroused. 'Now, Matt...'

'Now?' he teased thickly. But he was already moving lower to slide the scrap of white silk panties down her trembling thighs, stroking expert fingers to discover the honeyed warmth of delicate femininity. 'Now, Mrs Hawke? Before I've even unfastened these delectable silk stockings and suspenders?'

'*Matt*!' She was beside herself with desire. Swamped by sensations. They swirled and closed over her head like dark water; burned through her like black fire. 'Stop teasing me... Just for once, will you take me seriously?'

'Oh, I'll take you, sweetheart.' The laughing groan was ripped from him as he abruptly spread her beneath his weight, his fingers caressing the satiny flesh above the lacy stocking tops, levering muscular thighs between hers. 'I'll take you so seriously, you'll never leave me again.'

The savage tenderness of his possession rocked her like a storm breaking over her; made her tremble convulsively to the depths of her soul. She clung to him blindly, perspiration sheening her body—sheening Matt's too, under her seeking fingers.

His heavy invasion of her body was the physical release she craved. But the ravishing sensation of Matt's lovemaking was emotionally everything she wanted—everything she would ever want, she thought dazedly, and then she ceased to think at all. The storm swirled to a violent high, and then shuddered and broke in wave upon wave to flood her fathoms deep in delight...

'Tomorrow we'll go back to Skopelos,' he murmured, ages later. She was heavy-eyed, languorous, snuggled in sleepy abandon in his arms. Clinging to the present moment like a dream which might evaporate at any moment, she let the waves of velvet-dark sleep engulf her. Tomorrow... Tomorrow they had to talk about this. But tomorrow seemed a long way off...

'I got your solicitor's letter this morning.'

Matt, in denim cut-offs and loose black T-shirt, was braced at the wheel of the small powerboat they'd hired, his eyes hidden by sunglasses. They were skimming so fast over the waves that the bows of the launch were thudding dizzily up and down. The spray was flying, soaking her swimsuit and short white cotton sundress as she sat on the stern seat.

The sensation was exhilarating, and slightly alarming. She held on tightly to the sides of the boat, and watched the rugged coast of Skopelos rush by in a blur of green and blue and gold.

'How did it reach you?' The wind caught her words, whipping them from her lips.

'Sorry?'

'I said, how did it reach you?' She stood up, and climbed forward to stand beside Matt. 'Can we slow down?' She finished up wryly, 'It's hopeless talking to you when you're trying to break the world water-speed record.'

With a twist of a smile, he cut the throttle slightly.

'My housekeeper in Hampstead sent it to my poste restante address in Athens—Alexis's offices, in fact.'

'Oh.' She sought for something to say, but found herself lost for words.

'So now it's official,' he said, his expression bland.

They'd turned into the shore, and were nosing slowly into a small sand and shingle cove. Becky gripped the low windscreen of the boat and struggled to read Matt's mood; struggled to analyse her own. Since they'd woken in bed together in Athens earlier that day, there'd been an uneasy atmosphere of wary calm. She was too bewildered to think straight. And Matt was being too polite. She realised that she had no idea what he was thinking, what he was feeling…

'This is the taverna,' he was saying, cutting the engine and jumping knee-deep into the shallows to haul the boat to a safe mooring. 'Do you recognise it?'

She shielded her eyes and looked up the beach. Isolated, in a position which defied any custom at all, was the tiny open-air taverna. And at least half a dozen people were eating beneath the striped shelter of the bamboo awning. Behind, there was a goat, tethered in the shade of a gnarled olive tree. Higher still rose the olive-clad, thyme-scented hillside. The hot blue sky glowed behind the bright green pines on the ridge. The peacefulness was almost tangible.

'I recognise it,' she agreed, keeping her voice cool. 'We came here three years ago...' Why did she have to be such a jelly inside? On bare feet, carrying her white espadrilles, she picked her way up the beach after Matt. There was a natural spring, channelled into a makeshift shower at the top of the beach. She rinsed the salt from her legs, memories crowding back with agonising clarity.

'Remember the amazing feta omelettes?' Matt was watching her with an oblique smile.

'How could I forget? He makes his own feta cheese from his goats, doesn't he?' She gave a short laugh. 'Matt, why have we come here? You said you had something to show me.'

'I have.' He seemed to hesitate a fraction, uncharacteristically. His dark features revealed a glimpse of uncertainty. She felt her heart lurch. She was mystified, confused, and, after last night's impulsive surrender, painfully conscious of her vulnerability.

'Do you want to see it before or after lunch?'

'Now?' she suggested, with barely suppressed impatience.

'I'm ravenous,' he said, the uncertainty vanishing in a glitter of a smile. 'And it's quite a climb. We'll eat first.'

'Matt!' Half furious, half laughing, she followed

him into the taverna. The omelettes were exactly as she remembered—light, crunchy, delicately salty, irresistible. The wine was chilled, white and fragrant from the slopes of mainland Greece. The Greek salad was one of the best she'd tasted, full of juicy black olives from the hills of Skopelos.

The relaxed atmosphere and the intense tranquillity of their surroundings formed a stark contrast to the underlying shimmer of tension between them. Last night's abandoned lovemaking kept sliding insidiously into her mind. Whenever she met Matt's eyes over the table she had a vivid picture of her passionate surrender in their Athens hotel room, and felt herself go hot all over.

When the meal was over, and Matt ushered her wryly out of the taverna and towards a steep path between the olive trees, she felt almost too sapped by emotional stress to climb anywhere.

The bushes and dry grasses scratched her legs as she followed him. The shrilling of the cicadas filled the air. Breathless, she reached the top at last, where Matt had stopped. There was nothing there—pines throwing jet-black shadows in the brilliant sunlight, a wide flat area of bushes, more cicadas, intense heat. Nothing else.

'Here we are. What do you think?'

'Is this some kind of joke?' she demanded uneasily. Matt had flipped off his sunglasses. He was watching her with narrowed eyes. The blue of his gaze was intensified by the brilliance of the midday sky.

'Not at all. Look at the view…'

She turned slowly. The view was indeed breathtaking. The inlet of sea was azure, bordered by emerald pines, trimmed with the white-gold of the shore. A yacht with pure white sails was slowly sliding into sight. Further out, round the headland, a Flying Dolphin was skimming fast across the horizon, bound for the mainland.

'Yes, it's a nice view,' she agreed evenly. 'What are we doing here?'

'It's mine,' he explained, his tone suddenly abrupt. 'I bought it about eighteen months ago. When I still thought there was a chance that you'd come back…'

'You bought what? The *view*?'

'This stretch of land,' he corrected her patiently. 'I've got preliminary permission to build a house here. If you hadn't filed for divorce, I'd hoped we might design a place together. Have it built here.'

'*Here*?'

His face was completely deadpan. Not a flicker of emotion showed in his hard features.

'You don't like it? Too quiet? Too far from the big city lights?'

'Don't be silly.' Her voice sounded unfamiliar—faint, husky with shock. She was struggling with her reactions, trying to comprehend what he was saying.

'Or I could have it built further down there, nearer to the cove. I own the cove too. And the hill. And the olive groves...'

She was shaking her head slowly, bewildered.

'*You*?' she managed weakly. 'Owning hills, coves, olive groves on a Greek island?'

'It used to belong to a goatherd and his family. Some Germans bought it all from them about ten years ago. They couldn't get enough return on the olives, so they sold it to me.'

She stared at him for a long time. There was a rock behind her, with a flattish top and a basking lizard. The lizard darted out of sight like lightning as she slowly sat down.

'So...eighteen months ago,' she began, her throat dry, 'you came to Skopelos, bought this land...?'

He nodded. His eyes on her flushed face were so hard and intent that she felt as if he could probe inside her head.

'And then what did you do?'

'I sold my companies. Extricated myself from my directorships. Devised a plan for a change of life-style.'

'Because of me?' She hardly dared ask. Her voice came out as an uneven whisper.

'What do you think?' That brilliant gaze was annihilating her composure. The hard mouth quirked in bleak amusement. 'Didn't I tell you what a powerful lady you were, Mrs Hawke? What else can a man do after his wife walks out on him?'

She bit back a short, nervous laugh. Cautious, wary happiness was fizzing through her veins. But trusting Matt didn't come easily...

'Quite a lot of less drastic things, I imagine.'

Matt came slowly across to the rock. Carefully he sat down a few inches away from her. She caught her breath as his knee brushed against hers.

'Becky, you might have thought that I didn't even notice you leaving me. You were convinced I was partying in Hong Kong, having an affair with Su-Lin? I wasn't. I never had an affair with Su-Lin. Su-Lin's family were quite keen on my marrying her, it's true; so was Su-Lin. But nothing was ever officially agreed.

'And from the moment we made love, that night in London, you were the only woman in my life. I know you don't believe me; you never did. Just like you wouldn't believe me on the phone that night when I told you that letter was Su-Lin's last ditch attempt to cause trouble. Meeting up with Su-Lin in Athens was a clumsy attempt to show you that you had nothing to fear from her...'

'Nothing to *fear* from her?' she echoed faintly. 'She looked as if she wanted to *eat* you.'

Matt's eyes flickered with bleak humour, but his intent expression didn't alter.

'The feeling wasn't mutual. And that's the way

things were when you walked out. After you left, I went into shock,' he said wryly. 'I worked my way rapidly through from shock to rage, from rage to denial, from denial to finally understanding what a stupid bastard I'd been—'

'Matt…'

'There's something that happened to me that I never told you about,' he went on hoarsely. 'And when I thought about it, after you'd left, I decided it had a lot to do with the whole hellish mess I'd got us into. There was a girl at university. We were both just eighteen. We were in our first year; we fell in love in an immature, calf-love sort of way. I really cared about her. At the end of our first year, she failed her prelims. She took an overdose, and died.'

'Oh, no…'

'And I decided that the popular pastime of falling in love was an activity to avoid at all costs. I'd already seen what falling in love did to my father…'

'I'm so sorry.'

'It was so long ago, Becky,' he explained tersely. Twisting round, he took her hand. His tanned fingers felt strong and warm. She shivered involuntarily at the reaction she felt, simply at the touch of his hand.

'That happened to me thirteen years ago. I hadn't forgotten the girl, exactly, but things like that sink to the murky bottom of your subconscious. It wasn't until I started analysing why I'd handled my relationship with you so badly that I realised I'd been defending myself from real commitment. I'd let myself care about someone once, and the outcome had hurt. Do you understand what I'm trying to say?'

'But when I told you I was pregnant, you asked me to marry you straight away,' she whispered, her heart swelling at the shadow of wary masculine emotion in his eyes.

'It was a convenient excuse,' he admitted huskily, his eyes bleak. 'Bringing a baby into the equation was something to hide behind. I could fool myself that I was just doing my duty. I loved you so much, I was appalled at the prospect. When you asked me not to go that night, outside Sofie and Richard's house…do you remember?'

She nodded slightly, her teeth digging into her lower lip.

'I remember.'

'You were the one woman I really wanted, and I was so scared that I couldn't get out of there fast enough. I nearly lost my sanity in Hong Kong, thinking about you.'

'I still don't understand… Matt, if you cared about me, why did you leave me and fly off to Hong Kong when I needed you? When I lost our baby.' Abruptly she was crying. The hot tears were running down her face. Her heart felt as if it might burst.

With a sudden fierce movement he raked his fingers through his hair, then dropped his hands to rest on his spread knees. His face looked gaunt as he gazed into her eyes.

'Yes, I really screwed that up, didn't I? I thought you resented me. The so-called reason for our marriage had gone, hadn't it? Ted Whiteman had told me you'd hated giving up your modelling career for pregnancy.'

'*Ted* said that?'

'At our wedding-reception in fact.' Matt gave a twisted smile.

'That's just ridiculous,' she said huskily, dashing away the tears with a shaky hand. 'I loved the idea of having your baby. I stopped modelling because I wanted to. Just like I quit my studies because I wanted to. Maybe…maybe it was a bit immature and naïve, but all I wanted to do was to be Mrs Matt Hawke. I was so in love with you…'

Matt's face was bleaker. Under his dark tan his face looked white and strained.

'Ted Whiteman seemed very confident of his facts.'

'I suspect he did have a bit of a crush on me,' she admitted slowly. 'He must have been deliberately stirring up trouble. I didn't know. I never gave him the tiniest bit of encouragement. Do you believe me, Matt?'

'I was so bloody insecure, I believed *him*. And I already felt guilty about you giving up your degree course. And then suddenly we'd lost our chance of a baby, and we were looking at each other like strangers. I panicked. I could see our relationship getting to the point where it was going to hurt like hell. So I jumped on the next plane…'

There was a long, charged silence. Finally, Matt said expressionlessly, 'Let's suppose we didn't get divorced—'

'Matt, I—'

'Let me finish.' Underlying the deadpan tone was a hoarse intensity that silenced her. 'Let me outline the way I see things, Becky. I still own the house in Hampstead. I intend to spend some time in London each year. I'm planning to rent a house here temporarily, in Skopelos Town, while I think about building this place up here.

'Financially I'm pretty self-sufficient; I sold enough companies to keep the wolf from the door for the foreseeable future and I've whittled my work commitments down to the extremely lucrative part-time consultancy with Alexis's set-up. I'll need to be in Athens once a week, maximum.'

'How did you manage that?' Matt's logical, practical analysis of his new lifestyle and his dogged determination to paint a rational picture of a viable future were intensely moving. Her throat felt tight with emotion. She felt as if she'd been punched in the stomach.

'I helped them on some take-over deals that they were involved in a couple of years ago.' Matt's tone was casual. 'When I approached them as a financial consultant they were gratifyingly eager to bite my hand off. But I've a couple of other business interests over here.

'And I plan to dabble with these olive groves, and the little taverna down there on the beach, and do some fine weather sailing, but generally devote ninety per cent of my time to being a great husband. What do you say? In principle.'

She stood up. Suddenly the shining prospect of saving her marriage to Matt was there before her, and it seemed so unreal, so unexpected and unlikely that she couldn't take it in at all...

'Can we go back to Skopelos Town for coffee?' she managed lightly, avoiding his eyes. 'I'm roasting up here...'

'Of course.' His tone was painfully ironic as he led the way down. 'I wouldn't want sunstroke to be added to the rest of the charges against me.'

The short trip back in the launch was taken in uneasy silence. Being with Matt, with this unspoken tension thickening the atmosphere, was like riding an ominously quiet tiger.

As they moored on the quayside and climbed up the ladder to the pavement she glanced at Matt uncertainly. It was her move, she reminded herslf, drymouthed with nerves. Matt had gambled and had set out his cards. It was just a question of climbing over

the barrier, of contemplating the breathtaking risk of
opening herself up to the pain of loving Matt again.

'Do—do you have some plans for the house?'

'Only preliminary ideas. They were on the boat,
so they'll be a touch soggy,' he said, with a wry
grin. 'But my architect has a set, so all is not lost.
Shall we have coffee up at the Old Mill?'

'Fine.' She nodded, wincing at the stiff politeness
between them. 'There'll be no one there, but I've
got the key to the kitchen.'

Keeping a formal distance between herself and
Matt's tall, prowling figure, she walked along the
quay, past the crowded cafés under the shady mul-
berry and plane trees, past the rows of ice-cream-
coloured boats with their masts tinkling in the
breeze.

The steps up to the Old Mill were steep, but she
realised that she was feeling fitter than she had for
a long time. She was hardly out of breath as they
reached the deserted terraces of the restaurant and
paused to admire the view. It was mid-afternoon—
siesta time. A sleepy silence lay over the brilliant
white walls, the purple shadows and spills of hectic
pink bougainvillaea.

Becky let herself into the small round kitchen
with her key and made them both coffee.

When she emerged, Matt was sitting at a table
where there was a dizzying view down to the harbour. There was an aura of coiled tension about him,

despite his lazy body language as he casually tilted his chair backwards to a near-dangerous angle.

She joined him, placing the dark green coffee-cups carefully on the table between them and following his gaze down over the low wall. Uneven, old grey slate roofs and red pantiles fell away below, in a jumble of ancient, whitewashed Greek walls. The sun was scorching hot, tempered by the breeze. A lean-looking grey cat was perched on the edge of one of the roofs, living dangerously, precariously washing its face.

Becky squeezed her eyes shut, then opened them again, blinking in the sun. She had that despairing sensation of drifting away from Matt again, as if nothing she could say would ever bridge the rift. It was a panicky, frightening feeling. She stirred her coffee with a shaky hand. Was it pride? Caution? Whatever it was, it felt like an invisible strait-jacket that held her back from throwing herself into his arms and voting for reconciliation.

'I do hope Sofie and Richard can stay here,' she said quietly.

'Is that a heavy hint, Mrs Hawke?'

'If you like.' She looked at him uncertainly, and saw the bright gleam of humour in his eyes. Her heart gave an annoying jerk of response. She loved him so much, she realised belatedly—so much that he could abandon her again and again, have affairs with half a dozen Su-Lins, and she'd still love him…

'I don't think there's much doubt about them staying, now that I'm their new sleeping partner.'

'You are?' Her face lit up, her throat husky as she added quickly, 'Oh, Matt, that's wonderful news. When did you agree it all?'

'Richard and I tied up the legalities the morning we got back from Skyros.'

She caught her breath. Her coffee-spoon dropped into her saucer with a clatter.

'Before we went to Athens?'

'Right.' The dark features were cautiously mocking.

'So...that threat you used to make me come was just a—a—'

'A ruse? Yes.'

'Matt!' She began to stand up, her temper rising. 'First the sailing trip, now this? How can I ever trust you, when all you do is play tricks on me? What kind of basis is this for a marriage—?'

'We're together, aren't we?' he cut in softly. His wary grin fired her anger and touched her heart simultaneously, 'Instead of thousands of miles apart. That's not a bad basis for a marriage.'

'Matt!'

'Cool down; look at it this way. Everything I've done, since you walked out on me, I've done it for you. I wanted you back. I wanted our marriage back. Fair means or foul, Becky, that's the truth—all I wanted was you. If you can't see that; if you can't see how much I want you, then I'll have to keep on thinking of ways to make you see. Hire another boat, maybe. Kidnap you again…'

'No…I… It's all right,' she managed unevenly. She sat down again. Through her indignation, there was a stubborn, resilient glow shining right from her heart, melting her pride. 'I do see.'

'You do?' Matt's gaze was disturbingly brilliant under his heavy lids.

'Yes!' she agreed, a touch breathlessly. 'And… and speaking of your boat, it *will* be repairable, won't it?'

'So the boatyard says.'

'I feel bad about that. I'm sorry, Matt…'

'Me too.' He stood up abruptly, and came around the table, pulling her to her feet. A shudder went through her as he stepped closer, and slid his hands down her back to mould her to him from breast to thigh. 'Although, I've got a confession to make, Becky—it wasn't my boat.'

'*What*?' She stiffened incredulously, glaring up at him, and he tightened his hold. The narrowed gaze above her was as blue as the sky.

'Then whose was it?'

'I borrowed it from Alexis.'

'You mean to tell me… All this time you've let me believe I've smashed up your…your nautical pride and joy, and it was just *borrowed*?'

'Does that make it OK?' he teased softly. 'Smashing up someone else's boat? At least I took the blame for you in the nightclub.'

'Oh, Matt...' It was no good—abruptly her flare of outrage died and the funny side was unavoidable. She found herself laughing. Once she'd started she couldn't stop.

Laughing too, he pulled her into his arms and kissed her. She stopped laughing and kissed him back, with an intensity that made him break for breath and thrust her back, with lidded, teasing eyes.

'Never kiss me like that in a public place,' he reprimanded her, 'unless you want to land me in a Greek prison for indecent behaviour.'

'Luckily there's no one around,' she whispered, clinging to him hungrily. The dramatic reaction of their body-contact was scorching right through her, even hotter than the sun shining down from the clear blue sky.

'What do you want to do, Becky?' he murmured thickly, his face in her hair. 'Name it, sweetheart. I'll fix it for you.'

'What I'd like to do is help you design that house on the hill and...'

'And...?'

'And spend the foreseeable future just being Mrs Matt Hawke...'

'What about your career plans?' he murmured, crushing her closer.

'While I was in Africa I decided that I'd like to

work with children,' she whispered. 'But with a bit of luck they could be our own, couldn't they?'

'So, can we shred your solicitor's letter, feed it to the fish in the harbour, and resurrect our marriage vows, Becky?'

'Yes. Oh, yes, please.' She was trembling and laughing in the blissful strength of his arms.

'One more question.' His voice had hoarsened, the rasp of desire unmistakable as he moved her harder against him. 'Since "with my body I thee worship", Mrs Hawke, would Sofie and Richard mind if I invaded their house and your bedroom and made love to my wife for the next forty-eight hours?'

'No... In fact I suspect that they'd be nearly as pleased as I would.'

Her whisper was shaky with love and laughter as Matt's lean fingers linked fiercely through hers and they began to walk down the white-washed steps together, in the warm shadows of the afternoon...

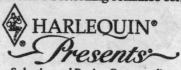

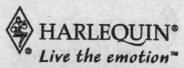

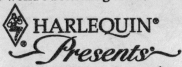

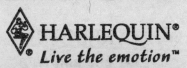

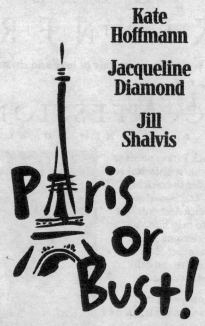

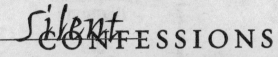

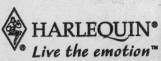

COOPER'S CORNER

Welcome to Cooper's Corner....
Some come for pleasure,
others for passion—
and one to set things straight....

Coming in May 2003...
FOR BETTER OR FOR WORSE
by Debbi Rawlins

Check-in: Veterinarian Alex McAllister is the man to go to in
Cooper's Corner for sound advice. But since his wife's death
eight years ago, his closest relationship has been with his dog...
until he insists on "helping" Jenny Taylor by marrying her!

Checkout: Jenny has a rare illness, and as Alex's wife her
medical costs would be covered. But Jenny doesn't want a
marriage based on gratitude...she wants Alex's love!

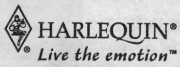

HARLEQUIN®
Live the emotion™

Visit us at www.eHarlequin.com

CC-CNM10

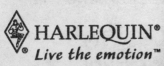

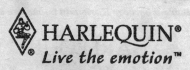

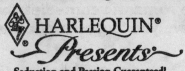

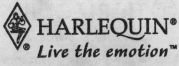